The Only Gift

OLIVIA SHAW-REEL

God, I thank and love You.

To my family and supporters—my "Libby Loves"—who continuously love on me and my books, you have been the GREATEST gifts to me, year after year!

To my husband, Paris Reel, for the beautiful cover design and encouragement—thank YOU!

-*OSR*

PROLOGUE

Heavy rain caressed the rooftop of the contemporary-styled home that sheltered a single, half-sleeping occupant. A thunderstorm was brewing in the November night; it was evident in the dark, rolling clouds, and faint rumbles coming from the Heavens. Plus, the weatherman had mentioned the seasonal anomaly on the morning broadcast. Still, nothing could have prepared the young woman, nestled cozily between cotton sheets and an oversized T-shirt, for the jolt that went through her body as thunder clapped like a Baptist church choir.

She shot up in bed, her dark hair piled on top of her head in a messy bun, and stray tendrils sticking out in all directions. Her chest heaved up and down as though she had just come from running outside, and sweat accumulated at her hairline. With eyes now widened in fear, she looked around the dim room and hated her negligence in not leaving a nightlight on. The blankets that were once tucked beneath her delicate chin were now a puddle around her hips, and the heels of her palms kneaded into her eyes roughly, daring the sleep and confusion to leave.

She'd had a nightmare. It wasn't her first one and likely wouldn't be her last. The sounds of gunshots were still echoing in her mind, and if she hadn't dreamt them so vividly, she would have almost believed the chaos had taken place in her home just now. Thank God it hadn't. She exhaled a shaky breath and both hands dropped robotically at her sides. Something had to give. She couldn't go on like this.

Her eyes darted to the orange prescription bottle on her nightstand, where it seemed to whisper her name. Though she had not unscrewed its white top and swallowed its small pills in weeks, she knew tonight would be the night to start up the old routine. They were sleeping pills, and if she wanted *any* success for her workday that began in just four short hours, she knew what she had to do.

A bottle of water with about a third of liquid left was planted at her bedside, and with a few long gulps, she had slipped the medication past her tongue and down her throat, wincing as it took effect immediately.

She settled back into a position that was comfortable and would carry her through the wading storm and seemingly never-ending night. But the gesture was done only after she plugged in a nightlight and double-checked the locks on her doors and windows.

Maybe one day, she'd have a good night's rest without the pills and without the nightlight. Maybe one day she wouldn't be so afraid to close her eyes and relax. Maybe one day she wouldn't have to look over her shoulder and worry about her safety or sanity.

But   today   wasn't   that   day.

CHAPTER 1

"**W**elcome, welcome, WELCOME to the Elm Grove Elementary Father-Daughter Dance! We are so excited to have you here this evening. Everyone looks SO lovely!" Principal Schumacher raved over the staticky microphone, his baldhead gleaming under the gymnasium lights.

More than 200 first and second graders stood around in combinations of pink, red, and white, and were made up in lipsticks and eye shadows that were much too mature for their ages. If Bryson McBride never saw another frilly dress, ruffled pair of socks, or oversized bow in his life again, he knew he'd be okay. Still, he wouldn't trade his place at his niece's side for the world.

Junie was—hands down—his favorite first

grader, wearing a red, age-appropriate tutu, a white camisole and a pink blazer with red hearts stitched on the back. She moved effortlessly from side to side in her chunky, strappy heels, and the light blush that was applied to her rounded cheeks shimmered. Her hair, which reached mid-back when straightened, was curled loosely and held out of her face by a sparkly, red headband that left glitter everywhere she moved.

Of all the titles and hats he wore—former marine staff sergeant, volunteer peewee coach, brother and son—the "Uncle" title seemed to be his favorite by far. It was moments like these, spending time with his niece and stepping in for her deceased father, *his* brother, that made life worth living. Plus, her compensation of sweet kisses, bear hugs, and piggyback rides, was also nice.

A popular hip-hop song took over from the slow jam and pumped through the speakers. Its lyrics were squeaky clean and edited and rightfully so, and made all of the exhausted children perk up again. Girls near and far grabbed the hands of their fathers, brothers, and grandfathers, and scurried to the dance floor. Meanwhile, his Junebug, as he affectionately called her, took that as an opportunity to sit down.

"Whew!" She crossed a leg and wiped the back of a pudgy hand along her forehead. Sweat beads gave her a flushed look. "I am TIRED! Can we take a break?" she whined.

Bryson settled beside her, chuckling and resting an arm along the edge of the lunch table that had been setup for wallflowers and pooped partiers. He nodded at an older man across from them, who looked to be dozing off while his granddaughter danced to the song overhead. Bryson smiled warmly, turning back to his date.

"You deserve a little break. You've been dancing for like..." he checked his watch, "...twenty minutes straight. Want some water? Punch?"

"Mmm," she thought long and hard about it,

but he knew exactly what she'd pick. Punch. "Fruit punch, please."

Yep. He knew her well.

"I'm going to get you a glass. You okay sitting here by yourself or you want to walk with me?" He held out a hand, again, already knowing her answer.

Junebug was sassy and independent at home, but was shy and introverted in public places. She grabbed his hand instantly.

"C'mon! I'll lead you to the table."

He chuckled again, following her lead, though he'd previously spotted the refreshment table from where he stood. It wasn't hard to see much of anything, as 95 percent of the people in the room were less than four feet tall. They eased through the sea of dancing bodies, some keeping in good rhythm while others looked lost and lacked energy as the night marched on. The scent of cologne was thick throughout the gym, mixed with the lighter, sweeter aromas of fruity perfumes and the dance's choice entrée, pizza.

Bryson had shamelessly downed three slices to his niece's one and a half, and they'd sipped on water at the start of the night. They both deserved a sugary drink and cookie from the dessert table.

"Havin' fun, Junie?" he asked.

She looked over a shoulder, nodding with the signature side grin he loved so much on her. Her curls bobbed around her head, falling back into their rightful places.

"Uh huh! Can I have TWO cookies?" She expertly batted her eyelashes.

Junie was a little on the plump side, much like her mother, and her weight was oftentimes the reason for being bullied. As of the start of the school year, her mother and doctor insisted that she cut out breads and sweets. He personally thought she was perfect and healthy, so for tonight, she didn't have to stick to any diet plan. This was *Junebug and Unc's special night*, as she'd referred to it so many times.

"Yes, but…." he lowered his voice as he leaned in, his eyes twinkling with mischief, "You have to keep it between me and you. Don't tell your mom."

Her eyes lit up. "I won't. I swear!"

"Don't swear." He gave her a wink, loosening the bowtie around his neck a bit and standing back to his full height.

There was an assortment of chocolate chip, oatmeal, sugar, and cranberry nut cookies, all spread out neatly. While she picked out the cookies of her choice, Bryson surveyed the gym for the hundredth time tonight. He took in the large balloons blowing from the overheard fans, the streamers perfectly placed and draped, the flickering strobe lights, wall-to-wall men with their special little girls, and…and…

Bryson's eyes widened slightly, locking on the retreating figure of a woman. In fact, she was the *only* woman in the building old enough to drive, vote, and run for president.

"Good God Almighty. Who is *that*?" The words were pushed through his clenched teeth as though he were in pain. His eyes followed the woman, much like many of the other father figures in the room. It was not because of the mermaid dress she sauntered in, her hips and backside swaying and seemingly keeping in rhythm with the bass of the song. It was not because of the expensive looking jewelry pieces along her neck, wrists and ears that gave off an air of class. It was not even the makeup that was professionally and delicately painted over her features. It was the captivating hazel-brown eyes, button nose, high cheekbones, cinnamon skin, and smile that caused Bryson's breath to catch.

He careened his neck even more, watching as she walked up to a few of the children and hugged them. "Junebug...who is that?"

Cookie crumbs fell from her mouth and her eyes squinted. "I can't see over all these people," she whined. "Who are you pointing at?"

He hoisted his niece up into his arms, her hands holding snugly onto his forearms. "That lady, there! *Her.*"

"Oh!" Familiarity shone in her eyes and a toothy smile nearly split her face in half. "That's my favoritest teacher in the whole wide world! She works in the library and she helps out my class at recess and lunch sometimes too. Miss Foster! Miss Foster!" Junie's voice was lost over the hum of the crowd as he lowered her back to the ground but at least he knew *who* she was.

"She's beautiful," he breathed.

"Oooh, *Uncle B's got a girlfraaaand; Uncle B's got a girlfraaaand!* I'm tellin' Miss Fooooster!"

Bryson grabbed his niece by the back of her blazer when she began to skip in the direction the teacher had gone. "Hey, hey, hey. I thought we were cool. I thought we were here." He moved his index and middle fingers back and forth, from his eyes to her eyes. "You can't be telling on me. Just like the cookies. That's our little secret, okay?"

Junie giggled, swaying back and forth. "I'm just kidding. All the boys in my class think she's cute too." She shrugged. "Uncle B?"

"Hmm?"

"I've gotta pee."

He stepped to the side. "Lead the way to the bathrooms. I'll hold your snacks for you."

Five minutes later, Bryson leaned with one foot propped up against a row of army green lockers. He held his niece's half eaten cookies in one hand, wrapped up in a napkin, and her cup of juice in his other hand. She'd also insisted he carry her little blazer, so that was draped around his arm. He chuckled, knowing she had him completely wrapped around her little finger and knew there was nothing he could do about it.

He heard a toilet flush faintly and stood upright, prepared to greet Junie again with a smile and playful "took you long enough," but he froze in his steps as the door swung open and out walked the librarian. The sweet fragranced, freckled nosed, plump-lipped librarian. She was even prettier up close, if that were even possible, as she wiped her wet hands on a napkin. Why did she look so familiar?

Miss Forest. *No!* Miss Faucet. *Definitely not. Ummmm.* Miss…

"Foster," he blurted and caused her to backtrack. "Miss Foster, hi," he repeated.

She smiled at him. "Hi, how's it going? Have we met?" She discarded the napkin in a trash bin, her smile widening.

"No, I don't think so. My um…my niece is here with me. I only knew your name because she says you're her favorite teacher."

Bryson could kick himself, stuttering and sputtering over a woman. Hey, who could blame him? She was a very sexy librarian of a woman, though. Sheesh. She was stunning, and her unwavering eyes did not help the situation whatsoever.

He forced back the thoughts and offered a charming half smile. "I'm Bryson, her uncle."

Miss Foster's eyes took in the cookies, fruit punch, and girly blazer with an amused sparkle. A dark eyebrow lifted. "You're the uncle of whom?"

"Oh! Right. Junie. Junie McBride."

"Juuuunie. Yes! I love her. We were just in the bathroom talking about you. She said she was here with her father, though."

"Yeah." He nodded in understanding. "I'm all she's ever known, but I'm her uncle."

Miss Foster's eyes looked him over again, but this time appreciatively. He did look dapper, if he said so himself. His broad upper half bore a charcoal grey suit jacket, and a black shirt beneath. His slacks were also black, fitting to his muscular legs. Keeping up with the color scheme of the night, he wore a deep red bowtie around his tattooed neck, a black and red paisley handkerchief tucked in his front jacket pocket, and black and red dress socks that could be seen with the right movement of his feet. He was the epitome of what *well-tailored* meant.

Bryson cleared his throat when she stared for a few more moments, her eyes widening and then falling to the floor.

"It was very nice meeting you, Bryson. I see your hands are full; otherwise, I would've, you know, shaken your hand."

"Understandable." He chewed at the corner of his full bottom lip unsurely, fighting back a smile as she seemed more flustered now. "You look really familiar."

"I doubt you know me," she said quickly, fidgeting. "But I said the same thing when I saw you in the gym."

"Is that why you were staring just now?" he blurted, unable to help himself, an amused smile on his lips.

Her jaw *literally* dropped, causing blue gum to fall out, and her gorgeous high cheekbones lifted. "Don't flatter yourself. I—I wasn't staring." She leaned to pick up the gum and tossed it sheepishly into a trash bin. "Though, I could say the same thing about you in the gym. I was always taught it's not polite to stare, you know," she teased.

Bryson shrugged coolly, his eyes skipping over her face and body quickly. "I was *definitely* staring. It's no secret. I mean, let's be real. Teachers didn't look *this* good when I was in school."

Miss Foster blushed. Bryson licked his lips. An awkward silence prevailed.

Junie's timing was working in his favor tonight, as she emerged from the double doors of the washroom, looking frustrated and upset. "I want to go home, Uncle B! Now!"

Both adults turned and eyed the young girl immediately. Bryson pushed away from the wall. "What's the matter, baby girl?" He noted the unshed tears, quivering lip, and flushed face. "Are you not having fun?"

She sucked in a deep breath, looking from Bryson to Miss Foster, up towards the ceiling, and then down to the floor. She scraped her heels back and forth. "As I was pee-peeing, I couldn't hold up my tutu all the way and…and…it fell in the toilet! Now I'm all wet and everybody's gonna laugh at me!"

Sure enough, Bryson saw the forming puddles below her feet.

"Plus," she added sheepishly, whispering, "I pee-peed on myself, too."

Miss Foster dropped down to Junie's level, grabbing her hands gently. Bryson watched the way the woman's eyes and voice softened, matching Junie's tone. "Honey, nobody's going to laugh at you. They won't even know what happened because I'm going to go in my closet upstairs and see if I have some extra pants or skirts up there that you can wear. How does that sound?"

Junie's eyes lit up and her lip didn't tremble as violently. "Oooh, can I go with you?'

Miss Foster stood up and looked over a shoulder at Bryson. "If it's okay with your uncle, sure."

Bryson nodded with approval. "We can go

upstairs but did you still want your cookies and drink?"

She shook her head left to right once. "Nuh uh. No thanks. I've had enough sugar for the night."

He tossed the food in the trash bin and followed behind the two who were holding hands like old friends. "Can we take the elevators? I've never rode them before," he heard Junie ask.

"You ride the elevator at my place all the time," he chimed in, but quickly shut up when she whipped around with attitude and sass.

"*Not* the ones at school, though! They're different!"

The adults chuckled. "Of course you can ride the elevator, honey. I refuse to walk up three flights of stairs in these high heels," she teased, rubbing Junie's back and leading her down the dimly lit hallway. "Unless, of course, you're going to give me a piggyback ride?""

"I'm too little to do THAT, Miss Foster!" Junie gushed and giggled.

"Oh, alright. I guess. Elevators, it is."

As they neared the third floor library, Bryson looked around at the bulletins, hand-drawn pictures, and other fun poster board projects that were decorating the lengthy corridors. Everything about the images screamed innocence, budding dreams, and big imaginations. It was clear some students were natural artists with their elaborate sunsets and houses and cars, while others opted to draw stick figures and basic shapes.

The empty floor smelled of crayons, old textbooks, and general staleness, as most schools smelled. His hand ran along the lockers while a grin splayed goofily across his face, spying one of Junie's masterpieces on display. He observed her handprint turkey for a moment, as keys were fished out of Miss Foster's handbag and the library was unlocked.

Miss Foster flipped on the light and motioned them inside. Much like the woman, her room was well put together and smelled amazing—like cinnamon and vanilla and everything else in the world that was feminine and sweet.

"Have a seat. The school closet is over here." She made a beeline for a door at the back of the room that was covered in construction paper and handcrafted leaves in different colored hues. "I'm so thankful that people donate to it. You never know when you'll need it," she explained before disappearing inside.

Bryson nodded thoughtfully, nudging his niece. "Junie, remind me to donate some of your old clothes and shoes."

Miss Foster's voice was muffled as she called out. "Would you like pants or a skirt to wear?"

"Ummm..." Junie looked up in thought.

"Whatever can fit me," she answered with a shrug, soon becoming distracted with a few of the books on a swiveling rack.

Both Bryson's and Miss Foster's laughter floated throughout the room. He felt a little silly sitting in a mini chair at a mini table, so he stood up and walked towards the corkboard beside her desk. His eyes scanned the photos of what he assumed was her pet Chihuahua, diplomas from middle school and high school, a 4x6 photo of an unknown woman with dark eyes and dark hair, and then finally, a portrait of a curly-haired, four-eyed kindergartner with an Ivy Carson Elementary School logo off to the side of the 5x7 image.

"No way," he whispered and blinked and then swallowed hard. "No...way." He picked up the photograph, traced his fingertips along the little girl's image, and then chuckled lightly.

"Okay, so we've got these..." Miss Foster emerged with three pairs of clean, gently used stretch pants and a dress with the tag still dangling from it. "Whaddaya think, Junie?"

Bryson turned, a knowing look in his eyes now and a crooked grin on his features. He saw Junie's *most favoritest teacher in the whole wide world*, in a whole new light.

"Camryn Young."

Miss Foster froze as the two words sank into the atmosphere. One could hear a pin drop the way silence unfolded. She looked over at him in surprise, her eyes darkening, as her government name rolled off of Bryson's lips. She dropped everything she held and nearly fell to her knees with them. "Wh—*what* did you just call me?"

"Camryn Young. I knew you looked familiar." Bryson cocked his head to the side and smiled even wider. "We attended the same elementary school; we were in the same daycare, preschool, kindergarten, and first grade classes before my family moved halfway across the country."

She reluctantly tore her eyes from his, swallowed so hard that it sounded painful, and then squatted down to pick up the garments she'd dropped. Her hands shook involuntarily and the pants slipped from her hands for a second time.

Bryson continued to talk and walk forward with bewilderment. "Tell me you remember me." He bent down to pick up the clothes and reached out to touch her arm cautiously. They stood up together slowly.

"I remember you."

"Do you really?"

She nodded. "I do. I remember your eyes especially. So mature and beyond your years," she whispered.

The adults inched forward, oblivious to Junie who was lost in her own world of books, building blocks, and imaginary friends.

"I got in trouble and the whooping of my life when I beat up Bobby Meyers for messin' with you," Bryson continued.

"He cut my hair." She subconsciously touched her own locks, fighting back a smile.

"I remember." Bryson scratched his temple while flashbacks of them as four, five, and six-year-olds flooded his mind. He stepped back a few paces, allowing his mind to wander and pick up the pieces over the last 20 plus years. "You were my very first girlfriend in first grade. We made it official under the monkey bars."

"I remember." It was her turn to fidget and reminisce. "Then, just before spring break, you gave me a candy ring. I accepted your proposal to be your wife." She giggled.

A tender smile touched his mouth. "We were each other's..."

"First kiss," Miss Foster—*Camryn*—finished off

quietly, clutching the clothes to her chest.

She began to say something else but Junie had glanced over from reading to a row of stuffed animals and let out the loudest, "EWWWW! You KISSED each other?"

"Hey, hey, watch your mouth." Bryson warned, looking over at his inquisitive niece. "And uh…remember what I said earlier about the cookies?"

Junie nodded.

"Don't tell your mother about this either." Bryson winked and without another word, stepped across the colorful rug that had all sorts of shapes and squiggly lines on it. He gathered Camryn in his arms, gently picking her up until her feet were off the floor, and then spun her around. "It's good to see you, girl. Wow!"

Camryn's eyes closed and for a third time in the last five minutes, the clothes fell from her arms as she returned his hug. "It's great to see you too, Bryson. I can't believe it took me this long to recognize you."

They rocked back and forth, whispering endearments in the other's ear, and then pulling back to chuckle with their foreheads pressed together. She began retelling a funny story how Bryson's hand got caught in their first grade classroom's fish tank, when Junie walked over and interrupted.

"Can someone PLEASE e'splain to me what's going on *here*?"

Bryson and Camryn jumped apart, looking down at the defiant little girl glaring up at them with her hands on her hips. They looked back to one another, smiling goofily again, and then burst into a fit of giggles.

After changing into warm, dry pants and returning to the dwindling dance downstairs for another half hour, Bryson could see the fatigue on Junie's face. She was sleepy and wanted her uncle all to herself. She was tired of sharing him with her classmates who thought he was the coolest thing walking the earth's surface. So when she pleaded for ice cream, he obliged and gathered all of their things to leave.

Camryn, who had only dropped in to be a backup chaperone for the assistant principal, had also grown exhausted and needed a break from her heels and tight dress. He offered to walk her out to her car, which happened to be three cars down from his. She retrieved a pair of ballet slippers from her trunk while Bryson tucked a sleeping Junie into his backseat. She snuggled up to the warmth of an old coat he had lying in the back. He dropped a kiss to her forehead and closed the door.

"I guess that means more ice cream for you," Camryn joked, tugging her heavy earrings off and dropping them into her handbag.

"I guess so." He shoved his hands in his pockets, rocking back and forth on the balls of his feet. "Cam, I can't say it enough. It's really good to see you—to see you're doing well and looking amazing, by the way."

"Same to you. Thank you." She ran a hand up her other arm, rubbing it for warmth. "It's a big step up from the glasses, bad hairdos, and snaggleteeth, right?"

"You were *always* pretty to me," he reassured. "I just have one question though."

She raised her eyebrows.

"*Foster*? Are you, um, married now? I mean, I didn't see a ring, but…"

Camryn looked around into the night, her face an orangey glow from the streetlights. She leaned in closer and lowered her voice. "We should talk about this some other time, some other place."

"And when would that be?"

Her eyes rolled upward and widened as she pondered the question. He realized this was a look of concentration she had developed over the years. It made for a cute expression.

"I don't have any special plans for tomorrow or Thanksgiving, or Friday for that matter. We can always do Saturday morning, too."

Bryson thought about his own schedule. "I'll be hosting my family over for Thanksgiving, if you want to come. And if not, I understand. Otherwise, I will see you Saturday if you're not too tired from shopping for Black Friday deals," he joked.

"With what money? I mean, I *am* on a teacher's salary after all," she kidded back. "See you soon, B."

He felt silly saying this, but needed to know. "I need your number."

"Oh! I uh, I slipped it in Junie's purse when she was changing clothes. You'd better call me too," she spoke pointedly.

Bryson chuckled and rubbed his hands together. "You're a slick one."

Camryn only smiled mischievously, wiggled her fingers a few times in a goodbye, and then got in her car. He watched her pull off into the night before getting into his own vehicle. A quick peek over his shoulder revealed that his niece was still asleep and lightly snoring with her thumb in her mouth. He frowned a little, vowing to talk to her mom about that. He would hate for her to damage her teeth by sucking her thumb.

With a permanent and downright goofy smile on his face, he twisted the fob in the ignition and took off down a deserted road to his sister-in-law's house. Too tired to do much of anything else, he promised himself that he would remove his clothes and head straight to bed once he dropped Junie off.

His plan was underway and off without a hitch, a half hour later, as he shuffled into his bedroom and collapsed between the linen sheets. Moments before he succumbed to sweet sleep, his phone shrilled through the silent night. It was just past the 11 o'clock hour, but all the important people in his life knew nine o'clock was the cutoff point for phone calls and text messages, unless there was an emergency.

He almost prayed to God that there was an emergency since his body had pretty much given into fatigue. His legs ached from Tootsie Rolling with Junie and his arms were a little sore from the multiple midair spins he'd performed with her. All he wanted was sleep. All he *needed* was to close his eyes to become dead to the world, but something prevented that. His darn ringing cell phone. He searched just below his pillow for the buzzing phone, resisted the urge to throw it against the wall, and glared at the unknown number.

He slid his thumb across the screen to accept the call. "I swear to God if you're a telemark—"

"Bryson," a woman breathed in relief, her voice sultry and soft.

His eyes popped open and he cleared his throat. He could remember that tone anywhere, anyplace. "*Camryn?*" He licked his dry lips. "Is everything okay?"

"It's Skylar," she rushed to correct. "Skylar Foster from your daughter's school. I'm sorry to call so late but I wanted to see if you'd like to meet for breakfast tomorrow morning? I know it's last minute."

His eyebrows bunched together in confusion. He pulled the phone from his face, looked at it, and then put it back up to his face. "Uh, yeah—yeah, Cam...I mean, uh, Skylar. Sure. I don't follow you with the—"

"Meet me at my place, okay? I'll text you the address in a little bit."

"Okay, cool." He strained to hear her. "Are

you sure you're alright?"

"I'm fine. Have a goodnight," she spoke hurriedly, and then hung up even quicker.

He sat with the smartphone to his ear a few more moments, eyes still leveled with the ceiling and perplexity pumping through his veins. He was so puzzled that he forgot the most important matter. *How had she gotten his number?*

CHAPTER 2

The next morning, his car eased into a cozy cul-de-sac and drove up into the driveway that matched the address she'd text him.

"Talking about a teacher's salary. She's doing well for herself," he mumbled, squinting up at the geometric home. What surprised him most was that she was only five minutes from Junie's school. In fact, at the right angle, he could see the top of the three-story elementary building from her driveway.

He shuffled out in sweatpants, a T-shirt, and boots, huffing into the cold November air. He snatched his sweatshirt from the passenger seat and yanked it on. It took him only a few seconds to walk briskly up the slanted driveway, being sure to pull the skullcap down to cover his slightly reddened ears. He had almost forgotten how cold winters in St. Louis could get. *Almost.*

Camryn's short frame appeared in one of the oversized windows when he rang the bell, and her smile warmed his insides instantly. He couldn't help chuckling at the way she waved quickly and then bounced out of sight. The sounds of shuffling could be heard before the door swung open and she stood before him, comfortable pajama pants and a tank top on, and cute little mismatched socks on her feet.

Camryn was fresh-faced and looked the complete opposite of what he had seen the night before, but this particular look wasn't bad. It wasn't bad at all. She was beautiful and comfortable in her own skin, and he appreciated it. When he didn't say anything, she tilted her head and shivered involuntarily at the blast of cold air.

"Good morning! I'm so glad you could come."

She grabbed his large hands, tugging him inside. "Now get in here! It's freezin', and you're letting all my warm air out!"

"Thanks for having me. How did you sleep?" He discarded his boots on the welcome mat.

"Pretty good. I got about five hours in before I went for my run and then watched a few sports highlights."

"Sports highlights?" His eyes practically shot up into his hairline. "No offense, but I didn't take you for a sports fan."

"I'm a very big basketball fan, probably bigger than most dudes you know," she added, whisking past him.

He couldn't help notice how her hips swayed in the same hypnotic cadence as last night. He forced his eyes to focus above her backside and beyond her shoulders at the interior of her home.

"Oh...my."

He followed her through the echoic foyer and towards the open concept kitchen and living room area. Hues of brown, cream, and beige screamed at him, while stainless steel appliances and strategically placed decorations offered a touch of femininity. His eyes moved up and around, down, and then around again while he nodded slowly, appreciatively. "*Very* nice home. You live here by yourself?"

"This is all me, yep." She nodded, following the direction of his eyes with pride. He was looking at the high-vaulted ceilings and admiring the sun-touched portions of the room as the natural light shone through her wall-to-wall windows.

"Cam...this is beautiful." His eyes dropped back down to where she had settled on one of the stools surrounding her chestnut island countertop.

She sipped from a mug, watching him over the

brim thoughtfully. "Have a seat. Can I get you something to drink while the biscuits finish baking? I've got coffee, orange juice, water—"

He circled around her, and nudged her gently with his elbow. "I'll have whatever you're sipping on. It smells good."

"I have pomegranate green tea."

He gave a disgusted look and mounted the stool across from hers. "Orange juice is fine."

She giggled and twirled around to dig around in her massive, side-by-side stainless steel refrigerator. This was perhaps an unfair assessment, but last time he checked, teachers didn't make enough money to afford these kinds of luxuries. She poured him a glass and slid it his way on a coaster.

"Thanks."

"You're welcome. Thank *you* for coming over.

I wanted to talk more with you last night but Junie was sleeping, you looked tired...and yeah, that wasn't really the place."

"What's on your mind? I have to admit, your phone call confused me last night." He took a sip of the orange juice, visibly relaxing when he didn't taste any pulp. In his opinion, pulp could ruin any drink for him.

Camryn sighed, and her eyes left his to look beyond his head. An almost pained expression crossed her features and he noticed immediately the way she began picking nervously at her nails. "I know there was some confusion with my name and things like that. It's a *really* long story, but..."

Bryson noticed her darting eyes and looked around. "You waiting for someone?"

"No, why do you ask?"

"My eyes are down here, Camryn. Relax, girl. What's going on? Here. Come sit down."

"No, I have to watch the biscuits."

"Come. Sit. Down." His stern tone did the trick as she settled in the stool beside him. That didn't stop her hands from fidgeting. "*Now* you can tell me what's wrong."

Camryn rubbed her hands over her face and then peeked at him through her spread fingers complete with well-manicured fingertips. "Between me and you?"

He nodded and reached out to gently pull her hands down. His thumbs rubbed the backs of her hands soothingly. "Between me and you."

She exhaled. "Okay, well, about seven years ago, I was working as a bank teller in Louisiana while I finished up my undergrad. I was working a Saturday morning shift that I wasn't even on schedule for, but I needed the overtime and agreed to switch with a coworker."

Bryson nodded, absently rubbing his hand

over the condensation on his cup.

"I went in and opened up at eight, did my normal thing of preparing drawers with the manager. We were talking, laughing, and just having a good time while we waited for our morning rush. But there was something different about this day. I felt really weird, you know? We had only serviced about two or three customers; it was storming out, and the day just dragged on and on." She closed her eyes, going back to that day, her voice changing slightly with the looming emotions. "I—I can't even explain it, Bryson, but I *knew* something was off."

He reached out to grab her hand again, not sure what she would say next but knowing she needed reassurance to go on.

"Around noon, just as we started counting out the drawers and closing up for the day, this guy came in with some of his friends. They were dressed funny and acting weird. I recognized him as one of my classmates at Grambling, but he'd dropped out like a month before. They—they busted through the door, laughing and being obnoxious, and asked me if I could help them with something. The manager had gone off to the bathroom so it was just me out on the floor. I asked if they needed help, and my old classmate pulled out this creepy, scary Halloween mask and a gun. He told me I could help him by opening up the vault and keeping quiet."

Her hand grew tense against his, so he squeezed tighter, offering her strength and encouragement to continue.

"Of course, I was *not* trying to play the hero, so I did as I was told. By that time, the rest of the guys had put on their masks and pulled out their guns. All the while they're roaming around, I could hear them laughing and talking in these eerie voices. Speaking in code. Laughing hysterically. It was like a movie."

She coughed lightly and cleared her throat before continuing, "A few of them stayed near the door as the lookouts, while my old classmate and another guy hopped over the counter and…and…he put the gun to my back while I put in the code to the vault. I didn't get a chance to press the emergency button under the counter, and to this day I feel so guilty about what happened next. I—I…" Her voice broke as the emotions of that day overtook her. She pulled away from him and backed away, hugging herself.

"I never mentioned to them that I wasn't the only one in the building, and I wish I had. My manager came from the back, from the bathroom, and screamed. I guess she shocked everybody. The first reaction from my old classmate was…he—he um…he turned around and without even thinking, just…he…"

Bryson's eyes closed briefly, understanding with a heavy heart. "He shot her?"

She nodded, tears streaming down her face, and her complexion paling slightly. Her eyes locked with his. "He shot her! He shot her MULTIPLE times like she was nothing. Like she wasn't a mother…like she wasn't someone's daughter…someone's sister. Someone's friend.

MY friend. He just killed her, Bryson. I can't get over that!"

He stood up and moved to embrace her, but she shook her head. She held up her hands shakily. "No, no…that's not even the half of it! I was forced to just turn away from my friend bleeding out and dying, and…and…I opened up the vault and told them they could take it all. I curled into a ball in the corner of the room, and begged for my life. I guess they weren't really there to kill, because as soon as they saw the money, that was the only goal. He called a couple more of his friends in to fill up some plastic bags and they cleaned the vault out. Took everything."

She sniffled and closed her eyes. "I kept my eyes closed the entire time and only opened them when I heard them running out. I didn't want to see anything else; I didn't want to see my friend on the floor; I didn't want the guys to even THINK I'd seen their faces or what kind of car they were driving, or what direction they drove in. I just wanted to close my eyes, fall asleep, and wake up from a very bad nightmare." She hiccupped. "That was just the start of my problems."

He attempted again to reach her, and this time, she allowed him to pull her in his arms that were warm, comforting, and filled with all the strength she didn't have in the moment. One of his arms was wrapped around her waist and the other cradled her head, much like he'd done many times with Junie.

He peered down at her, softening his voice, "Take your time. What else?"

She blinked with exhaustion, staring ahead at the lettering on his sweatshirt. "I didn't know this for another couple hours until the police informed me, but in the process of them fleeing, their getaway driver lost control of the wheel and plowed right into a woman and her child on the bus stop." She swallowed hard. "The crash killed them instantly."

Bryson felt his knees weaken just a little but

couldn't show that he was affected. She needed him to be her strength.

"Of course," she continued, thick tears cascading down her cheeks again and rounding off at her chin. "The robbers kept going. So not only had they taken one of my best friends from me, but also they'd caused more heartache for ANOTHER family. I—I couldn't be silenced. I had to speak up. I was asked to provide a statement and my account alone had the power to put them away for a long time. I agreed to testify and because it was a federal crime, which resulted in three counts of second-degree manslaughter, it was recommended that I be placed in the Witness Protection Program."

Bryson's stomach dropped.

"Imagine that," she continued, shaking her head. "Twenty-two years old, uprooted from my home and my family and friends without so much as a goodbye, and dropped off in the middle of nowhere as a librarian in a suburban elementary school. I didn't get to complete my degree, and barely said goodbye to my loved ones. Only my parents were informed of where I was headed. My name was changed and for the last several years, I've lived as Skylar Foster."

Bryson could feel his eyes grow wider and wider, the more she shared. It was strange, but he felt an overwhelming need to protect her. He couldn't fathom saying goodbye to his loved ones and being abruptly placed in another city, in another state, and in another home, and being forced to start all over. He couldn't imagine going through life alone, much less the drastic changes she'd gone through, and he felt for her. Correction: his heart *ached* on her behalf. There were so many dreams put on hold and unfulfilled goals all because of another person's selfish and senseless actions.

Wrapped up in his thoughts, he barely heard her excuse herself until he felt her pull from his arms. She disappeared down one of the hallways while he turned towards the oven to check on the biscuits. A burst of heat smacked him across the face as he opened the oven door and retrieved the medium-sized pan with an oven mitt. He deposited the sweet-smelling bread onto the stove and tossed the green oven mitt into a drawer. He could hear her blowing her nose in the distance, followed by the sound of water running. His head throbbed with all of the information she had given him while he searched her refrigerator for butter.

Camryn took her time returning, not that he minded, so he used that time to butter the biscuits, fix a plate for each of them, and reheated her tea. The microwave was beeping when she reentered the kitchen, her face freshly washed and her eyes less clouded and troubled. She had also thrown on a little lip gloss and changed her shirt that had been moistened with tears.

"Feeling better?" He offered a small smile.

She saw what he had done with the food and breathed in deeply, inhaling the different aromas of bacon, eggs, and seasoned diced potatoes. "Much better. Thank you for setting up everything for me."

He took a long sip from his glass and their eyes met over the brim. "My pleasure. Thank *you* for cooking and sharing your life with me."

They sat in silence for a few moments, the room quiet and still, except for the clanks of forks to plates, or the swishing of ice and juice, and the ruffling of napkins.

"Can I ask you something? Obviously, you don't have to answer if you don't want to."

"I'm listening." She wiped her mouth free of bacon grease.

"So with the program, are you able to see your parents at all? Do you talk to them regularly?"

She smiled but it wasn't one filled with love, joy, or even humor. It didn't quite reach her eyes. "I haven't talked to them in…God, how long? Well, put it this way. My mother was diagnosed with breast cancer March of 2018, last I heard through a *cousin*, and my father passed away in his sleep three years back. I couldn't attend the funeral. In fact, the program FORBADE me to go back to my home state, so I got updates through emails from my family."

Bryson shook his head. "That's horrible, Cam. Your own father's funeral was off limits? I'm sure one day wouldn't have mattered, and someone from law enforcement could've escorted you."

She pulled a biscuit apart slowly, watching the steam billow from it. "I hear you, but that wasn't even the hardest part. When I first explained to my parents what had happened at work and that I was going to testify, they begged me not to. They called me selfish and every other name in the book, but I couldn't keep quiet. It would have killed me to let some murderers get away with what they had done."

"You have a good heart and always have. I'm sorry your family couldn't support you through that. I'm sure it was tough."

"Tough can't even begin to describe it, Bryson. I had no one; my family disowned me; I couldn't say anything to my few college friends, and I wasn't able to finish out the SIX credits I had left at Grambling. I was placed in one of the most conservative jobs out there," she explained sadly. "A SCHOOL library teacher, Bryson. Now, don't get me wrong, those children mean the world to me but I know God had something else in store for me. Sometimes I wonder if I made the right decision, and if the sacrifice was worth it. But then I think of my friend, and…and that mother and daughter, whose lives were cut short, and I'd do it all over again." Her eyes slammed into his with such force he almost fell off of the stool. She looked like a determined woman who had faced a bunch of hardships but had overcome them all.

"Your strength blows my mind, Cam. It really does." He shook his head, scooping up some of the cheesy eggs. "Are you allowed to go back home to Louisiana now that it's been some years?"

"I could, but I won't, and of course, it's always

advised not to. I would be considered a dead woman walking, as the D.A. puts it. The problem is, they're not even worried about my old classmate and his friends finding out where I live. They'll be locked up for a long time. It's more so their families and friends that pose an issue. You know, scorned mothers and vengeful family members are the *real* danger apparently."

He chewed thoughtfully. "And this information you're sharing, are you supposed to be telling me?"

"Not exactly." Her eyes dropped down briefly before she looked back up at him. "I know we just reunited after so many years, but I—I trust you and you represent everything about my old life that I miss. When you called me by my real name yesterday, I almost shut down. I haven't heard or used *that* name in years. As far as I was concerned, Camryn is dead and gone."

He shuddered involuntarily at the thought. "Paint the picture for me. I mean, I can't wrap my mind around this. You're here...alone...by yourself?"

"Alone. By myself," she repeated and nodded. "I can't get too close to people for obvious reasons. I keep it really short with coworkers; I just do my job, show love to the kids, and come on home. I can't remember the last time I went to a movie theatre or out to eat, or to the mall for clothes. Online shopping has become my favorite entertainment. I hardly ever leave this house except to run, or purchase groceries here and there, and every so often, I'll hit up a drive-through when I'm not up for cooking."

His heart dropped further. "You're like a prisoner."

"In many ways, yes."

"But you're not necessarily in danger here in St. Louis, right? Is it just that you're so used to looking over your shoulder and fending for yourself that you don't like going out and getting close to other people?"

"Exactly." She nodded slowly. "That's exactly right. It's just better this way, you know? Less to explain. Less to hide. Less to share."

Bryson rubbed his forehead where a headache was forming. "What um…what do you need from me? How can I make your life a little easier?"

She smiled slowly, gratefully. A sparkle entered her eyes as she reached over and grabbed his hand. "You can start by telling me what happened to you in first grade. Why'd you leave? That Friday, you were sharing a Lunchables with me and then Monday, the teacher was ripping down your name tag off your cubby."

Bryson pushed his plate away and stretched, feeling satisfied and full. She had grown up to be one heck of a woman and a great cook. He would have to get another free meal sometime soon.

"Lunchables, huh? I think you still owe me an Oreo," he joked. "Nah, but I don't know if you remember, but my dad was part of the Air Force, so we were travelling from base to base, up until his retirement. I was inspired to do my civic duties and joined the Marine Corps when I was 17. For 11 years, I served, moved up the ranks, and became staff sergeant over a squad of like 30 men."

"Did you say staff sergeant? What? You go, Bryson. That sounds really important."

"I did my thing, you know," he teased, tossing a wink in her direction. "I interacted with a bunch of soldiers and got to oversee most of the equipment operations. I pretty much had the job of making my soldiers the best soldiers they could possibly be, mentally, physically, and emotionally."

She shook her head in amazement. "You are NOT the little boy I remember. He was mischievous and had a short attention span."

Bryson threw his head back with a laugh. "Let's just say I wouldn't have made it to staff sergeant if I hadn't outgrown my short attention span. I wouldn't have made it past the recruitment process."

They giggled for a few moments.

"I am so proud of you." Her smile had faded by now but there was still amusement in her eyes. "Anybody who risks their life for others is a hero in my eyes."

He placed a hand over his heart and bowed his head dramatically. Then his eyes grew serious as he spoke his next words, "You just remember that the next time you ever get discouraged about your decision to testify. You're a hero too." He winked again.

"And what about the family? How's everyone? Any wife or kids?"

He almost spit out the last of his juice. "Wife and kids? The only things I'm committed to right now are sports and TV dinners." He tugged at his collar sheepishly. "As for Mom and Dad, they're both retired and living in Hawaii."

"*Hawaii?*"

"Yeeeah. Sometimes when winter hits, I wonder why I didn't follow them," he explained, smoothing his hand over his facial hair. "Warm weather and sunshine is all they're chasing these days. Between travelling and threatening me for grandkids, I'd say they're pretty carefree and in good health. Every few months I make the trip out to them so they can see Junie." He shrugged.

"And you have a brother if I remember correctly, right?"

"*Had.* Bryant passed in combat."

"I am so sorry."

"You didn't know; don't apologize. Junie is his one and only daughter, so I've been helping to take care of her since he died."

She smiled warmly and nodded. "She's in great hands. You do a great job with her."

"'Preciate it, 'preciate it." He tipped his head towards hers. "I'd like to think so."

"If you have to leave, don't let me stop you," Camryn told him, hours later, as they sat across from one another on her cream-colored couch. It was filled to capacity with mauve, coral, and tan pillows.

Bryson was leaned with his back against the arm of the couch, his long body stretched out towards her, and his ankles crossed. His arms were folded comfortably behind his head as though he was relaxing in his own home.

She also exuded comfort with one leg bent up and pressed to her chest, as the other was stretched out in front of his. Her chin rested on her knee and both hands were clasped in front of her bent leg.

"I'm enjoying this downtime quite nicely, thank you," he told her.

"I hope your feet don't stink, all up on my couch like that," she kidded.

He lifted one of his legs to tickle her side with his foot. She shooed him away unsuccessfully and laughed loudly, trying to dodge his foot with the limited space the couch provided. He assaulted her for a couple moments, enjoying the laughter that flowed from her pretty lips, and then brought his leg back down.

"Let me ask you a personal question."

"Uh oh. Cue the mysterious music." She lifted an eyebrow.

"Teachers don't make all that much. You have a home that...doesn't exactly reflect schoolteacher salary." Bryson motioned around the living room with a hand. "I mean, no offense whatsoever."

She nodded with understanding. "This is all thanks to my father's life insurance policy. He may have disowned me, but he kept me as a beneficiary." She shrugged. "Thanks, Daddy."

"And what about your name? Can I call you Camryn when we're together like this, or would you prefer Skylar still?"

It didn't take her long to think about his question as she faced him fully. "Please, call me Camryn."

He nodded. "One last question…"

"Shoot."

"How did you get my number? I know you mentioned sliding *your* number in Junie's bag, but I missed the memo about my number getting into your hands. Not that I mind, but…I just wanted to know."

She turned shamefaced, hiding her smile behind her knee. "I know it's not ethical, but I came home and thought about how good it was to see you. So I logged onto our school attendance database and looked up Junie's emergency contact information. Your name and number was there and I couldn't resist. I'm sorry if I disturbed you."

"No, no, I was just wondering. You scared me for a minute," he laughed. "I'm glad you called me though. I really am."

She blushed and whispered. "I'm glad I called too."

Bryson stayed over another few hours, so late that the sky began to darken into night and the moon slowly made its appearance.

"I can't believe it's this late. Now I *really* feel bad for keeping you. I'm sorry."

Bryson paused on his way out. He turned to cup a hand over her cheek and smoothed his fingertips across her smooth skin. He leaned down and pressed his lips to her forehead once and then twice, before giving her hand a squeeze.

"Stop apologizing. I wanted to be here, and I enjoyed my time. Those dishes and laundry waiting back home for me aren't going anywhere." He watched her eyelids close again and he couldn't resist placing another kiss to her smooth face. "I want *you* to get some rest. If you ever need me, you can call or text me any time, any day, okay? Please don't be a stranger."

She pulled her bottom lip between her teeth and then released it slowly with a nod. "Drive safely. And if I don't see you beforehand, have a wonderful Thanksgiving."

"Yeah, you too." He waved a goodbye.

CHAPTER 3

Bryson hummed along to some old school radio station he had stumbled upon as it played back-to-back 90s hits from Jodeci to SWV. He licked his fingers free of the rich cranberry sauce he'd spilled and twirled around on his heels, doing a little dance in the middle of the kitchen, and then proceeded to add more of the sauce to a bowl. He wasn't a big fan of it, but knew his family loved it, so he had purchased a can during a grocery run last week.

Today's menu was sure to add a ridiculous amount of calories to his normal 2,200-calorie diet. He expected to gain a few pounds, and for that reason, he'd worked out earlier that morning at the 24-hour gym in his building. In five hours, Bryson had whipped up creamy macaroni and cheese, deviled eggs topped with shrimp, tender roast with potato halves and carrots, and a medium-sized pot of mustard greens. His sweet tooth led him to the bakery section of the grocery store where he'd purchased a sweet potato pie the night before, and he cheated a little with the stovetop dressing that he preferred over the traditional kind. His sister-in-law, Briana, was bringing potato salad and banana pudding by. It was clear who was the better and more trusted cook for such an occasion, but he wasn't tooting any horns or pointing any fingers...*yet*.

His mind drifted back to a simpler time when his brother, Bryant, was still alive, and they would have little cook-off competitions. Who could bake the better cookies? Who could better deep-fry a turkey? During Christmas, they turned things up a notch and Bryant would make gingerbread cookies from scratch while Bryson made the gingerbread house. Their treats were always full of sugar and made with love, and it was a testament of how they had been raised to cook and fend for themselves. Their mother's motto was: *if you can cook for yourself, you don't have to wait until you're married to eat like a king.* God, he missed those moments. God, he missed his BROTHER…his best friend. Life hadn't been the same since that fateful July.

A timer went off on the stove, breaking him from his thoughts and indicating his final countdown. All of the dishes were done and steaming hot. He still had about an hour until Briana and Junie showed up, so he took his time setting the table and loading the few dirty bowls and utensils into the dishwasher. He hopped back into a shower, shaved off the five o'clock shadow he had been sporting, and threw on his holiday attire—a God-awful turkey sweater with oversized pajama pants that kept falling off his hips until he rolled them down twice.

His eyes locked on the festive picture Junie painted for him in art class. The floating stick people with their oversized interlocked hands and nonexistent clothes made him smile. She had painted her family and the things she was thankful for. He couldn't wait to see his baby girl after two whole days.

But when noon turned to one, and one became 1:30, Bryson grew worried. He called his sister-in-law's cell phone and received no answer. It was just Briana and Junie that he had been expecting, so there was no one else he could call. By 2:30, he had pulled on a coat and was heading from his building to stop by their house across town. He froze in his tracks as he saw Junie stepping from an unfamiliar car. He was prepared to yell and fight and defend her honor until he saw the woman leaving the driver's side.

Camryn.

What was Junie doing with Camryn, of all people? Where was Briana? Where was Junie's coat? Why hadn't *he* worn socks in these brisk temperatures?

His heart raced as he ran over to embrace his niece. "What are y'all doing together? Junebug, where's your mom? Camryn, what—what happened?"

Under any other circumstances, he would have made sure to tell her how good she looked, but couldn't do anything more than focus on his shivering niece. Camryn gave a tightlipped smile, motioning towards the building he had just bounded out of. "I think we should talk inside." She pulled her pea coat tighter, a look of concern marring her gorgeous features.

The second they were back in his warm, top-floor apartment, Junie leapt into his arms. Sobs racked her little body instantaneously. "Baby girl, what's the matter? Hmm? You can tell me anything."

She became inaudible as she cried openly and hoarsely. She was cold to the touch and her cheeks were rosy. He wrapped one of his blankets around her, rocking their bodies to a rhythm he not only prayed would calm Junie, but that would calm his racing heart as well. He suddenly felt very angry and confused. Helplessly, he looked over to Camryn.

"Why is my niece walking around without a

coat on and coming from your car? Don't get me wrong, I'm not upset with *you*, but she should be with her mother. They were supposed to be here almost three hours ago. Where is her mother, Camryn? Hmmm? Camryn, where is Briana? Talk to me before I lose my mind."

She nodded to all of his questions, understanding his disorientation, and clearing her throat. She stepped over towards their huddled bodies, speaking softly and carefully, "I stopped by the school to get some paperwork that I left. I have no idea how she knew I was there, but as I was walking out to my car, I saw her running up to me. I asked her what was wrong, she started, you know, crying like this. Just hysterical and unable to talk. Once I got her to settle down, she said her mom kicked her out so she could 'relax,' whatever that means. Thankfully, I remember you telling me you lived in this area, and when I came up Mason Street, Junie directed me to your building." Camryn sat down on the couch so she could rub circles along Junie's back but her eyes stayed on the fuming man to the left of her. "So, here we are. I'm just as confused as you."

Bryson saw red as his body sank completely back into the couch, pulling Junie with him. He didn't think it was even humanly possible until now, but he saw the crimson color and twitched from head to toe. He could literally feel his muscles tense up, and the bile in his throat rise. Suddenly, he no longer had an appetite for a Thanksgiving feast and all of the joy of the holiday had drained from his mind and heart. If Junie hadn't been nestled in his embrace, the wall would have been an immediate victim of his punches and kicks.

"She...did...WHAT? She—she KICKED HER OUT OF THE HOUSE?"

Camryn flinched. *"Bryson."*

Junie whimpered in his arms, burrowing further in the warmth his sweater and natural body heat provided. Camryn eyed him cautiously while he took a few calming breaths to compose himself. Only when he trusted himself to speak more rationally did he open his mouth again.

His hand smoothed over his hair while he growled lowly. "I can't believe this."

"Shhh. Take a deep breath for a second," Camryn encouraged softly, daring to touch his shoulder. "You're...it's like you're foaming at the mouth right now and your niece doesn't need any more stress. Please calm down."

Bryson's eyes closed briefly as he forced himself to breathe and think normally, willing away the violent and irrational things he wanted to do and say to his sister-in-law. They weren't appropriate in any way, shape, or form, and he almost felt bad for thinking them. Almost.

"Is this something her mom does often? I'm not following," Camryn added once she saw that his chest didn't heave as much.

He nodded shortly in frustration, his brows nearly merging together as a unibrow like he was in pain. He drew a hand up and rubbed the tension from his forehead. He had his own

The Only Gift

personal drumline going on in his head. "Whenever her mom says she needs to relax, that's code word for," he mouthed the next words, "getting high and shooting up."

Camryn placed a hand over her mouth. "Oh, my."

"How can somebody be so selfish? How can— someone...*anyone* kick their SIX-YEAR-OLD child out in these bitter temperatures, and go on like it's okay? She didn't even have a coat on! You know all the things that could've happened to her?" He spoke through gritted teeth. "Of course you know because you don't think like her stupid mother! I swear to God when I see her, I'm going to strangle her."

Camryn winced at his harsh words and realized the little person in the room didn't deserve to hear to any of what they were discussing. She stood up and peeled her coat and gloves off, and then held her hand out to Junie. "Hey. Why don't we get something to eat, honey? I know you were tellin' me you were hungry on the way over."

"She didn't feed you *either*? It's almost THREE O'CLOCK!" Bryson growled.

"Bryson, please!"

Junie rubbed her eyes with balled fists and then accepted Camryn's hand. She climbed off of her uncle's lap and followed Camryn to the bathroom to wash her hands and prepare for an early dinner.

Eventually, after calming down, counting to ten, and praying, he finally joined the girls around his rectangular table. He looked over Junie's disheveled appearance and grew angry all over again. Camryn noticed and gave a reassuring smile, motioning with her eyes for him to sit down while she warmed up everything again. She decided she would allow Junie to make her own plate so that it could take her mind off of what had just transpired. She could only imagine what was going through the poor girl's mind.

As Junie was scooping out some macaroni, her favorite dish *every* holiday, apparently, Camryn rounded the table and leaned in so that only Bryson could hear her words.

"I know you're upset, but this *is* Thanksgiving, and children remember how they felt on certain days, holidays, and in different moments. Please don't let this ruin the rest of your time together. She's already distraught and confused. Make the rest of the day the best you possibly can, okay? Please. For Junie."

He knew she was right and nodded. His fingernails picked at the placemat in front of him. "Yeah."

"Aren't you going to eat too, Uncle B? You don't have a plate," Junie pointed out, carefully carrying her plate with both hands and walking towards him.

He helped her into the chair beside his. "You know what, baby girl? I'm not even hungry anymore. I've lost my app——"

Camryn gave him a stern look.

"I uh, I'm going to eat what you're having." He gave a sheepish look.

"What about you, Miss Foster?"

Camryn smiled at the little girl's pleading, hopeful eyes. "Sweetheart, I'm not staying. I was actually going to go back home and...and..."

"But I want you to staaaay," Junie whined.

"No, no, enjoy your time with your uncle, honey."

Bryson looked over from piling his plate with roast, potatoes and carrots. "You're going home to do what?"

Her startled eyes locked with his. "Um...eat what I made and maybe have a few people over."

"A few people over?" He gave a disbelieving look and forked two devilled eggs, sliding them onto his saucer. He passed by her to place his cup and plate on the table, circling back. "Hey, Junebug? Give me and Miss Foster a second to talk. I'll be right back. Say your prayers and eat up."

Her mouth was already full of greens as she gave a thumbs up. Considering she was practically starving, he didn't make a fuss about her not saying her prayers before eating. He followed Camryn as she began pulling on her coat.

He chuckled in disbelief. "So, you're going with that line, huh? You know good and well you don't talk to people or have people over your house. You told me that yourself."

She tugged the belt around her waist that kept her coat pulled snugly together. Her hazel eyes refused to meet his. "It's complicated, alright? I can't just be hanging around with *my* student. How is this going to affect her at school? What if she slips up and says something that could get me fired?"

Bryson wasn't buying that for one minute. He scanned the length of her incredulously and then stepped forward to stop her when she moved to put her gloves on. "It's not a crime to have Thanksgiving dinner with someone, Camryn. Many teachers and students get together outside of school for tutoring and different things, so I'm not accepting that excuse. You told me yourself how you couldn't trust anybody and you don't think you ever will. In the past couple of days, you've managed to let me in, and you've let Junie in even further."

When she kept her head down, he leaned forward to study her face under the curtain of wavy, dark brown hair. One of his large hands reached for hers, rubbing the pad of his thumb against her electric skin. Their eyes met and he gave her a charming smile—one he knew she wouldn't be able to resist. "Just for the holiday, try to put your guard down and spend some time with people who enjoy your company. You *have* to eat, and I know you can't cook roast as good as I can," he teased. "Please? For me? Wait, no, do it for Junie. Think of the children, Cam. It's probably best you stay here and keep me levelheaded anyway. You know, with my bad temper and all."

She fought the urge to smile back, stepping away from the door and leisurely tugging her belt loose. He poked his bottom lip out and the battle was won. She smiled widely, giving in, as she watched him drop to his knees before her.

"What are you doing?" she giggled.

"I'm begging. I'm pleading. Can you please help a brotha out? I don't usually do this."

"Get up, silly. I'm staying. I'm staying. Geez, you're like one of the kids I teach." She eased out of her coat and hung it up in the walk-in closet of coats, umbrellas, and too many shoes to count. He took her in for the first time, appreciating how stunning she looked even in everyday clothes. He had now witnessed her dressed up formally, dressed down, and now she wore an off-the-shoulder mustard sweater that skimmed the waistband of her skintight, dark jeans. On her feet were leather, black ankle boots that zipped up along the sides.

Her hair was in its natural form—an array of naturally curly and wavy locks that had been combed out and then given up on. But the almost unkempt look was sexy, especially as she took a chunk and tucked it behind her ear that had thin gold hoops dangling from them. His eyes were drawn to her mouth involuntarily, stretched wide in a smile; she was still giggling about something. His eyes followed the length of her arm, as it dropped back to her side and then she propped her hands on her hips, spinning around.

When she faced him again, he watched her eyes light up in remembrance. "I remember…and *please* tell me you do too…during our K5 graduation rehearsal, Mrs. Machut told you that you couldn't sit by me because our last names were different. You told her you didn't care about the order but you only wanted to be with your best friend and she threatened to kick you out of the ceremony if you didn't start cooperating. You got a spankin' when your mom picked you up later that day."

His eyebrows knitted together as he reminisced, ultimately chuckling at the memory. "Surprisingly, I *do* remember that. Why you remember that is beyond me."

She smoothed her hand along his face, shaking her head with amusement. "Because that pitiful face you were just making reminds me of you as a five-year-old."

Bryson brushed his pants off and stood to his full height but not before stretching his back with both arms going in opposite directions. "Come to think of it, I don't know why schools have K5 graduations anyway. It gives kids false hope that K5 means the end of school. I cried so hard the summer after we graduated and my mom told me I had to go to first grade."

Camryn tossed her head back and laughed openly, picturing that day. "And you got ANOTHER spanking for throwing *that* little tantrum, right?"

"I did." He rubbed his backside and pretended to wince with pain. "Worst beating of my life."

They both doubled over in laughter until tears came to their eyes. The sound was so full of joy that one would never know Bryson had been ready to rip someone's head off just minutes before. As they continued to bring up distant yet fond memories, and worked their way towards the kitchen, Junie left her comfortable place at the table and peeked in on them. She smiled, watching her uncle and favoritest teacher in the whole wide world lean into one another for support while laughter flowed from their lips carelessly, boisterously. Their happiness brought peace to her young, troubled mind as she retreated back to the kitchen and finished off her dollop of cranberry sauce.

Completely oblivious, Bryson was the first to

sober up as he wiped the back of his hand across his eyes. "Man! It's so good to hear you laugh, girl."

"It feels good to laugh," she admitted. "Thank you for that and thank you for the dinner invite." She smiled down at Junie, running her fingers across the girl's head.

"Have a seat. I'll make your plate for you," he offered. "And don't complain when you see how much I put on it. I didn't make all this food for nothin'."

Though the day had started off rocky, this Thanksgiving Day turned out to be his favorite in a long time. They laughed, talked, ate until their stomachs ached, and played round after round of board games. Midway through the evening, he was able to get ahold of his sister-in-law's bum of a boyfriend and told them he would keep Junie the rest of the weekend. Bryson didn't ask any other questions and he certainly didn't reason with Briana about her negligence as a mother. He figured he would make the call quick in order to save his sanity and keep up his good mood, and then get back to the girls. Junie had her own room and a closet full of clothes and toiletries already, so spontaneous sleepovers weren't uncommon. He didn't mind spending more time with his princess, and she was excited when he returned from his call and told her the good news.

Junie begged for ice cream as the evening approached and decided she wanted to see a young Macaulay Culkin in one of his classic holiday movies. They gathered around the big screen in Bryson's bedroom with popcorn and mint chocolate chip ice cream surrounding them. Halfway through the movie, Camryn was out cold and breathing softly. She had been leaning into Bryson's side and had slid further down so that her head now lay in his lap.

Junie giggled, watching from the other side of him. "She must be really, *really* tired, Uncle B."

She attempted to whisper but it came out more of a laugh that caused Camryn to slightly fuss.

"She is. Shhhh. Let's go to your room," he whispered, quietly easing his thighs out from under Camryn's head.

He smoothed the unruly strands of hair out of her face and looked at her tenderly. She whimpered like she was dreaming and then smiled in her sleep. He could only imagine what she was thinking about now. She was absolutely beautiful in any setting, but especially now as her long eyelashes kissed the tops of her cheeks, and the way she unknowingly pouted her mouth. It was almost angelic the way her dark brown locks fell around her face, framing it gracefully. She'd let Junie braid and play in her hair half the evening, and now it had a messier, even *sexier* look.

"Uncle B?" Junie whispered, still standing in the doorway.

"Yes, baby girl?" He finished tucking the

blankets around Camryn, tiptoeing towards Junie.

She had her head cocked to the side in wonderment. "Why are you looking at Miss Foster like that?"

"Like what?" he mocked, fanning a hand across her face. She looked sleepy.

"Like...with sparkly eyes." She shrugged. "It's hard to e'splain."

Bryson pulled the door up so that Camryn wouldn't be disturbed and followed Junie into her room. "I didn't have sparkly eyes. I was just making sure Camryn was okay."

"Okay," she yawned, tugging her sheets and comforter back, unable to give any further reasoning in her sleepy state. "I'm tired." She yawned for a second time, stretching.

"You look like it. Change into your pajamas and put the clothes in the hamper. I'll be back to read you a story in a little bit."

"Okay," she said, even sleepier than before, sitting on the edge of the bed.

But when he returned, as promised, five minutes later, he had to chuckle because she had fallen asleep exactly where he left her. She was upright and her body bobbed from side to side as she slept. He walked over, pulled her shirt over her head and scooted her body back until she was relaxing into the pillows. She remained in her jeans and the tank top she wore previously, and proceeded to snuggle up with one of the fuzzy brown bears. He kissed her forehead and said a quick prayer of protection over her, thanking God for blessing him with such an amazing niece.

As he pulled away, a hand reached up to stop him. "Noooo. Lay with me," she murmured.

"There's no room for my big ole body, Junebug." He looked around.

"*Please*," she begged and he knew he couldn't say no. "Just stay until I fall asleep."

He looked down at all the possible places to lay—the twin-sized bed, the plush carpet beneath his feet, and then the rocking chair that had originally been in his grandmother's home. Bryson grabbed one of the pillows she wasn't using and a spare blanket from the closet. "I'll sleep here, okay? Get some rest. I'm not going anywhere."

She nodded and turned her body to face his; immediately, she succumbed to the slumber pulling at her. He planted his feet in front of him and rocked himself forward then back absently, wishing he could at least have something to occupy his mind from the lingering anger and the hopelessness of his niece's situation. Beyond wanting to give her a positive upbringing and being the best possible father figure, Bryson also felt responsible for not being able to help his sister-in-law overcome her addiction. Off and on, from the time that her husband—*Bryson's brother*—died, she had always depended on drugs and alcohol and other "quick fixes" to free her mind.

Bryson, on the other hand, always relied on God. He wasn't the most faithful churchgoer, but his relationship with The Man Upstairs was solid. He prayed often about any and everything, and knew he was so blessed because of God's grace, mercy, and unfailing hand. His thoughts consumed him until he could think no more, falling asleep in mid-rock.

He stayed in his same uncomfortable sideways position for a half hour, one arm tucked in his lap under the blanket, the other bent at the elbow on the armrest and his chin resting on top of his knuckles. A noise just outside of Junie's bedroom caused him to inhale sharply. Through his haze of fatigue and the thick darkness, he spotted Camryn as she stumbled out of his bedroom and rushed towards the front of the apartment. As quietly as he could, he shuffled through the blanket he was wrapped in and hurried to catch up to her.

"Cam...Camryn! Hold up." The stubborn blanket had gotten caught around his ankles, causing him to stumble. Camryn had completely stopped just outside of the door and was bent over, looking for her boots with the light of her cell phone, when he rounded the corner and clumsily plowed into the back of her. They both went crashing to the floor, and Bryson stuck his hands out in time to prevent his much heavier body from crushing hers.

With the air knocked out of her, he could feel the shake of her shoulders as she struggled to breathe and made some weird snorting sound. He realized quickly she wasn't in pain, but was laughing hysterically. "Oh…my goodness," she squeaked. "What just happened?"

"Are you okay?" He pushed upward and over, sitting up beside her and reaching down to help her up into a sit. They sat across from one another, their backs pressed into the opposite walls, their legs folded and chests heaving, their eyes sleep-filled and slightly reddened, and silly grins on their faces.

She rubbed the back of her neck. "You have a

HARD head. How did you even fall?"

"I was rushing and got caught up in this stupid blanket." He kicked at the fabric for emphasis but ended up ramming his foot against the closet door. "OW!"

Camryn clapped a hand over her mouth to keep from laughing and disturbing the only sleeping occupant in the house. His expression was funny, the situation was comical, and she felt giggly in her dazed state.

"Were you heading out?" he questioned once the blanket was worked from his ankles and feet. He helped her up, walking hand in hand with her to the front where she gathered her belongings.

"Yeah, I um...I apologize for falling asleep. I don't want to give you the wrong idea like I always stay the night at men's homes. I just...was really tired...and...the movie was softly playing, and..."

He squeezed her hand. "And you don't have to explain yourself to me. I think I have a pretty good idea of what kind of woman you are, and my respect and admiration for you is still just as high as it was before you fell asleep in my room. Stop worrying."

She visibly breathed a sigh of relief. "Thank you, and thank you for letting an old friend share the holiday with you. She really appreciates the kindness, conversation, and company."

"She's very welcome and I hope she knows she can be just more than an old friend. She can be a current one too."

Camryn grinned, her teeth brightening up the dim room. "She would like that. *I* would like that."

"Can I walk you out?"

"Oh, you're fine. Stay here in case Junie wakes up and…"

Bryson was already tugging on a hooded sweater and clumsily stepping into a pair of tan winter boots.

Hand in hand with little small talk, the pair headed outside into the night, where parked cars were glistening with light flurries, and the streetlights gave off an orangey-yellowy glow. The wind whipped around them and blew her hair in all directions as she pulled her keys out of her purse, and then turned to him expectantly.

He pulled her coat tighter around her, smoothed her scarf down around her neck, and then leaned in to embrace her much smaller frame. He ignored the sweet fragrance floating from her skin and hair and ignored the perfect fit of her in his arms. If he didn't, he knew the intoxicating scents would be engrained in his mind for days to come. He pulled back just enough to kiss her forehead and then released her completely.

"Text me when you make it home. Text me if you're bored. Text me…period," he told her.

"I will. Thanks again."

He winked and stepped back to watch her get in the car, buckle up, and then drive off with a wave. Only then did he head back up to the top floor to his place, and settled in his bedroom that still smelled like a woman. There, it was warm, cozy, and oddly lonely now that Camryn had left.

CHAPTER 4

Working out the day after Thanksgiving, or any major holiday, for that matter, was always fun because hardly anyone showed their faces after stuffing them with turkey, fattening sauces, and homemade desserts. Black Friday workouts were especially cool because half the city was asleep after shopping for an ungodly number of hours. He could have utilized his apartment gym, but there was something about the public gym, its rows and rows of equipment, loud up-tempo music overheard, and wall-to-wall mirrors that motivated him.

At Briana's panicked request, he had returned Junie back home to her, only after yelling at her for more than an hour about being a responsible, levelheaded, and *sober* mother. He gave her three weeks to attempt to get rid of her no-good boyfriend, try to find a stable job, and make strides to get clean of her heroin addiction. He knew realistically everything would take more time than 21 days, but he wanted to see just how serious and committed she was about taking back her life and making her only child a priority for a change. His brother was probably turning over in his grave now.

About a half hour into his workout, he had ditched the warm-ups and lifting for some cardio. He was running at a decent pace, his legs feeling sturdier than ever. Sweat poured down the sides of his face and the back of his neck, and his heart pumped healthily and vigorously. His black sweatshirt and undershirt had been tugged off and thrown somewhere beside the treadmill. Now all he donned was a bare chest, tattooed arms, and track pants that made a swish with each movement. This was proving to be his most intense workout in a while, as he burned off the carbs and calories from yesterday.

"Ah!" he hissed, feeling the burn...*loving* the burn.

His arms felt tight, his muscles felt strengthened, and…and yet his knees grew weak suddenly. His eyes had locked on the shapely figure outside of the window, walking briskly in the darkness and holding a basket filled with laundry. Camryn. He had grown to know that figure and her mannerisms quite well over the last four days. He had to chuckle at that. FOUR days in a row? God was definitely looking out for him.

His eyes followed her obvious ones as she entered the laundromat across from his gym. She locked the door behind her and settled at a washer furthest from the door. All he could see was the top of her head until she returned a few seconds later with coins in her balled fist. She pushed a few buttons, inserted the quarters and dimes, and then loaded her whites inside of the massive machine.

She had a washer and dryer at home; he had seen it with his own eyes. So why in the world was she out at a 24-hour laundromat at four in the morning?

Bryson ran several more minutes until he reached the six-mile mark, and cooled down with a couple stretches. After taking a quick shower and toweling off well, he changed into a clean pair of undergarments and a warm sweatshirt and matching pants that he normally wore on his grocery store runs, or when he wanted to be a lazy millennial playing his video games for hours. It was faded, with the U.S. Marines logo and mantra stamped across it, and the neckline was slightly warped from numerous wears. But he wasn't going to throw it away anytime soon, if ever. There were many memories in its scarlet and gold fibers.

He probably should have left her alone and given her space. She already looked paranoid and deep in her thoughts. But the other part of him was excited to enjoy her presence again, if only for a brief conversation of "hello, how'd you sleep?"

He threw on his large puffy coat, zipped it up halfway, and pulled the strap of his duffel bag over a shoulder. Long, purposeful strides took him across the street with his eyes on Camryn the entire time. Her head was down while she wrote in some sort of journal, so he tapped on the glass with a key. She jumped, startled, and looked around in apprehension. It was pretty dark out and contrasted with the brightness of the facility, she probably couldn't see much more than his coat and waving hand.

"Cam! Open up!" he yelled. "It's Bryson."

She couldn't understand him. He knew by her confused expression, but still, she made her way over. It took her a few tries, but finally, she unlocked the door and stood back as he shuffled inside. "Whew! It's cold out there," he spoke the obvious, stomping the light snow off the bottom of his boots.

"Thank God it's you." He heard from behind him, along with a deep exhale. "Can you...um, lock the door back, please?"

"Hope I didn't scare ya." He gave a reassuring look before doing as told. Somebody would be awfully bold and stupid to try to do something to them in the laundromat, especially with his towering size. Plus, he made no efforts to hide the weapon he carried at all times on his side. He mainly obliged to her question because her obvious fear of the unknown.

"Can I get some love?" He turned and opened his arms, asking for a hug.

She stood in front of him for a moment, admiring him from head to toe and smiling shyly, and then stepped forward into his thick, outstretched arms. "Hi."

"Hi," he mocked.

"What are you doing here?"

"I was working out across the street and saw you. What are *you* doing here?"

"You have a gym at your place."

"You have a washer and dryer at your house. We can play this game all day. Again, what are you doing here out all by yourself? It's the crack of dawn, girl."

She giggled and then sighed, backtracking to walk over to her belongings. He followed. "I'm not sure what's going on with my washer. I put a load in last night, woke up this morning, and there was still soap and water on my clothes, so I came here. Plus, I just couldn't sleep. I figured nobody would be out and about this early."

"Just us and God," he joked, his eyes scanning the empty facility.

"Are you doing any shopping today, or…?"

"I may go look for some electronics." He rubbed his hands together. "You know, a man can never have too many toys."

She rolled her eyes playfully. "Oh, Lord. Tell me you're not a video gamer."

"What's wrong with video games?" He gave her a sideways glance.

She groaned and then shoved her index finger in his chest. "I knew there was a flaw in you somewhere."

"Aw, what is this? So you thought I was perfect otherwise?" His eyes gleamed, matching her playful ones.

"I didn't say all that." She bit her lip to keep from smiling but ended up showing off her pearly whites and dimpled cheek.

"For real, what's wrong with video games? They help me relax after a stressful day. I'm not obsessed with them, but they're definitely up there in importance with my tooth brush, food, and my car."

"You'd better be joking."

"I am." He laughed.

"There's nothing wrong with them though. I just heard in my, um..." she fidgeted, "in the support group I'm in how wives of video gamers often feel underappreciated or neglected. Most of the women said they don't get much attention and they say how that's all the men seem to care about."

"Support group?" He lifted an eyebrow.

"It's online, yeah. It's a secret group for women and families who, you know, are in the *program*," she explained, fiddling with the detergent cap in her hands.

He nodded, growing quiet with understanding. "And how do you feel right now?"

"I'm okay. Got some good sleep, and..."

"No, no. I mean, being out by yourself. How do you feel? How did you feel when you decided to leave out this morning and come? This is a big step."

She chewed on her lip again, showing off that cute little nervous habit he had grown to love. "I can't believe I'm here honestly. I was paranoid. I felt like somebody, somewhere was looking for me, but…"

Bryson finished her thought, "But you survived and you lived a little. I'm proud of you." He gave a reassuring smile and fingered some of her hair that had fallen from its ponytail.

"Thank you." She sat down in front of her rapidly spinning washer, watching the clothes slosh around inside. He joined her, shrugging off his coat and stretching out across the bench comfortably so that his back was pressed into her warm side and both legs were dangling off the side. She moved her arm and he easily slid down so that his head could rest against her thighs. She giggled, looking down at his head and the fresh haircut he was sporting. He had to have cut his own hair; she didn't recall seeing it that way the day before.

"Comfortable?" she asked.

He watched her for a second before closing his eyes. "Very, and if you stay still, I could go to sleep right here."

"Mmm. I wouldn't suggest it."

"Why not?" His voice was dreamy, like he seriously was heading to sleep. He was only half kidding but she *did* have a warm, soft lap.

"Because I have to switch over the clothes," she said, seconds before abruptly standing and sending him falling back onto the bench with a thud.

He watched her in disbelief, giving her a pitiful look. He was enjoying this and so was she. A waft of vanilla hit his nostrils and lingered from where she'd been. "Oh, that's cold, Cam. That's how you do your boy?"

He watched her as she gracefully and shyly unloaded the clothes and then placed them in the dryer, adding coins and then a couple dryer sheets. He had never met a woman like Camryn and while he hadn't been around throughout their teenage or early adult days, he had to wonder if life caused her to be so calculated and conservative. Did her circumstances make her this meek, or had she always been so withdrawn? The way she laughed like she didn't want to draw too much attention; the way she smiled widely and then hid it with a hand; the way she blushed when he looked directly in her eyes—these were all pieces of her, so beautiful and so different than anyone he'd ever encountered.

He could rarely remember her personality being so layered when they were kids, but he appreciated the innocence. She was refreshing to be around whether she realized it or not.

When Camryn bent over to pick up a fallen garment, he respectfully looked away, clearing his throat.

"So, um, what's your plans after this? I don't think you ever said."

She turned from twisting on the cap of her laundry detergent and then rubbed her hands clean on her stretch pants. She sat back down beside him, their arms brushing lightly.

"I need to do some lesson planning, to be honest, but I don't see that happening until Sunday after church."

"What church do you attend?"

As close as he was, Bryson swore he saw a blush fill her perfect, melanin skin.

"I don't actually attend, but I log in twice a week and watch a live stream of a church in Dallas."

He nodded with squinted eyes. "What church?"

"New Age Trans..."

"New Age Transformation Church? Pastor

Rodney and First Lady Ayesha Hammond?"

She nodded slowly. "You're familiar with them?"

"They're my cousins," he said simply. "Well, Rod's my first cousin on my mother's side. I've known Ayesha for years. I'm the one who set them up actually."

"It's a small world. That's so cool, though. I love Pastor Rodney's style. He's very relatable."

"Always has been," Bryson agreed, looking down and smoothing his hands down his pants for warmth. "I remember we used to play around the backyard and he'd always get a sermon in. We used a couple of old boxes as the pulpit and sticks as microphones. We even snuck and put on my dad's ties once but after that beating we received for playing in his good clothes, we took a break from playing deacon for awhile. I don't think my butt ever recovered."

By the time he finished his story, Camryn had leaned over into his shoulder, chuckling. He loved her laugh. As her body calmed from the laughter and her eyes went back to their normal almond shape, and her lips formed a straight line, he noticed how she immediately went back to looking troubled. There was something on her mind.

"Hey, how long does the dryer cycle take?"

"About 40 minutes. I've got like 32 minutes left."

He stood up and shrugged on his coat again. "That's plenty of time then."

"For?"

He tugged on her hand. "I'm going to take you somewhere. Grab your stuff."

"We're going *outside*? What about my clothes?" She buttoned her coat, a shorter, more casual coat then the pea coat she'd worn over his house the day before.

"It'll be quick, like 20 minutes. We're just going across the street and we'll be able to see from there."

She looked unsure but she also appeared to trust him as she slung the lengthy strap of her bag across her shoulder and torso. "After you."

They walked to the gym he'd left not long ago. It was still empty and would probably be for most of the day.

"Why are we here?"

"'Why are we here?'" he repeated the question softly, but never actually answered, leading her past the rows of ellipticals, stationary bikes, and treadmills. He finally settled in the back of the facility where there were free weights, medicine balls, and punching bags. He let go of her hand and walked over to grab a pair of boxing gloves.

She stared at him, puzzled and skeptical. "What's going on?"

He laughed and tugged on her sleeve so that she could shrug off her coat and purse. While she stood before him in stretch pants and a graphic T-shirt that rode high up on her midriff, he couldn't help but to lick his lips appreciatively. Perhaps it was the change in scenery, the lighting, or the hundreds of surrounding mirrors, but he hadn't noticed her pretty, exposed skin back at the laundromat, or the way the fabric of her pants hugged her body just right. *Check yourself, bro,* he told himself.

"Relax, girl. Actually, I should be telling you to get ready. Put these on. We're about to punch some bags."

Her eyebrows shot up. "Okay, you've lost me. *What?*"

Bryson wrapped an arm around her shoulders and pulled her along to the punching bag. "You.

Punch. Bag. See?" He gave the 100-pound synthetic leather bag a good right hook with his bare fist. "Try it. You look super tense all the time and I know something's on your mind. So until you're ready to tell me what's bothering you, I'm going to let you punch away your frustrations and fears and insecurities."

"Bryson, I didn't come here to box."

"And you won't. You're just sparring."

"Bryson…"

"It'll help you clear your mind—all the stuff that's weighing you down," he suggested softly. "Come on, Cam. Just…ten minutes. Hit the bag for ten minutes, that's all. If you want to talk, that's up to you. But hit the bag. Give it all you've got until you can't take anymore."

Bryson watched as she chewed on her full bottom lip and shuffled her foot nervously. He tugged on one of the benches, maneuvering it so that he could straddle it and face her. Their eyes met in the mirror and he saw something click within her.

She spoke lowly, but it was loud enough to be heard over the programmed music. "It's crazy to me how everything sort of comes full circle. It's almost scary actually. I remember being little and afraid to speak up. This was obviously after you left and I had to have been in maybe second or third grade. It was like I'd been robbed of my voice. My parents thought I had become a mute. They thought something was physically damaged with my voice box and isolated me. They were ashamed of me, and left me at home a lot of the time because they didn't want anyone to know what a freak their daughter was."

She looked down, her eyes brimming with tears. When she glanced back up, she tapped the boxing gloves together and then drew her arms back, punching the bag. The bag moved slightly under the light force.

"Wanna know *why* I was so quiet and

withdrawn? My father's guy friend—my 'Godfather,' so he says—cornered me one night we had a family barbeque. I was instructed to stay in my room and watch TV. Isn't that something? Family was over, my cousins were running around, but my parents wanted me in bed early because I'd had a rough day at school that week so my Godfather brought up a plate and sat with me. He told me he understood why I was upset and said he would give me some company until my parents noticed he was gone. He...he told me we could play a fun game in a quiet place."

Bryson winced, already knowing what was about to come out of her mouth. Camryn's eyes closed and she blindly began punching the bag, steadily and with much more force than the first time.

"He put a hand over my mouth and told me to relax. Then he pulled me into his lap, and he molested me, Bryson! He molested me—an innocent, helpless little child. His Goddaughter!" she screamed. "When he was done, he told me I had to be quiet. He said that if I opened my mouth, he'd be in trouble and then I'd be taken far away from my parents. I had no idea what that meant! So I...I was quiet. I told no one. I kept that secret bottled up for FIVE YEARS until my parents finally put me in therapy. It took them FIVE YEARS to get me to talk and I still said nothing. Bryson, why was I so stupid, so naïve? Why didn't I tell on him and have the sense and courage to get him in trouble?"

Bryson moved to speak but she was in her own little world. She was now throwing punches that held more power and more impact and most importantly, she was talking and releasing all of the issues she'd been juggling with for so long.

"I thought my life was back to what it used to be. I thought everything would magically be right with the world again. I was talking again, making new friends, and my parents liked me again. They were no longer ashamed of me." She grew quiet, rubbing her gloved hands together nervously. "That didn't last long."

Bryson watched her wrestle with her next

words. "Why didn't it last?"

"There was this boy in my neighborhood. He was new to town and I befriended him. We walked to and from school together; he came over sometimes to watch TV or I went over to do homework or study. He lived with all guys, and his mom wasn't around. It was his two younger brothers, an older brother, and his father there. One day, I skipped school with him. We went to the mall and snuck in but were sent away after an hour because we were minors. We couldn't go to my house because the neighbors were nosey, and we couldn't go to his because his dad worked from home. He took me to a park and we walked around for hours, just talking, laughing, and enjoying each other's company. It was innocent, you know? There wasn't anything sexual about the time we spent together. He was such an amazing friend, and he listened to me. He...listened...to...me, unlike my father or mother. That was special to me. *He* was special to me."

Bryson noticed the way she said her last few

words as she pulled off her gloves one by one. She used the past tense bitterly. Her body became rigid and a rush of tears came, filling her eyes before cascading down her face. She let out a sound; it was a cross between a choke and a scream, before hitting the punching bag with both fists, faster than her previous punches, jabs, and hooks.

"They—they sent him away, Bryson! They just took him away from me!"

"*Who* took him from you?"

"My parents! They found out a couple days later that I had skipped school and waited for him when we got out the next week. They pulled us both aside and then they just," she hiccupped, "they told him how I had been in therapy, how I had to take certain antidepressants and medicines, and how I was a MUTE when I was younger. They told him getting involved with me would ruin his life and that I would be trouble. Know what happens next?" She laughed bitterly.

"He believed them."

"He believed them." She nodded, wiping the back of her arm across her watery eyes. "He was terrified of me after my parents were done talking to him, and that dissipated our friendship. It was over just like *that*," she snapped her fingers, "over some exaggerated truths. They took away my ONLY friend, Bryson. I kept to myself and went back to being quiet. I would speak only when spoken to and stayed off in my own little world. I didn't care about friends or popularity, or joining clubs and sports; I just went to school to learn and came home everyday."

Her punches lessened while she fought to catch her breath.

"Then fast forward to this mess with my parents and the Witness Protection Program, and having them blame me for being a good and honest person and reporting CRIMINALS to the police…and having them blame me for breaking up the family and disrupting their peace…and…and them not caring that I had

NOTHING AND NO ONE to start over with! How can they call themselves parents, Bryson? How could they say they loved me? That's not love!" she cried.

Bryson stood and walked closer, proud that she was speaking her truth, but also concerned that she had hurt her pretty hands without the gloves on.

"Shhh. Calm down. Come sit with me for a second."

She did as told, joining him on the bench while placing her hands in his much larger ones. He looked at her reddened knuckles. He leaned in to place his lips against them tenderly, hardly even thinking it through while the pads of his thumbs rubbed the backs of her hands.

"How do you feel now?"

She wiped her eyes and breathed in, releasing just a few more tears, before she exhaled shakily and then smiled. The corners of her eyes were moist but her smile lit up the room. She looked relieved, weightless. "Better. I—I actually feel better after doing that and expressing myself."

"Good. That was my hope. You didn't hurt yourself, did you?" He checked each hand thoroughly, gently turning them over and admiring each delicate finger. His touch was warm and lingering.

She blushed a pretty pink shade, and then swallowed hard, watching him as he watched her. "No, I...I should be okay."

Bryson nodded distractedly, resting their intertwined hands on his leg. "You've been through a lot, Cam. I don't know how you're still standing. Actually, I take that back. I know exactly how and why. May I?"

She nodded.

He placed his hand on her chest, feeling her

heart pump strongly and beautifully. "You have a beautiful heart and spirit, Cam. I know that and others know that. I just hope *you* know that. God has kept and protected you through a lot of situations that have ended in isolation and heartache, and it's amazing you are still so generous and loving, but it shows what kind of person you are. I admire that. You didn't allow your circumstances to harden your heart. You didn't allow your parents' opinions to deter you from living YOUR truth, and standing up for those people with no voices. Yes, it changed *your* life, but it also brought justice. You moved forward with your life; you made the best of your situation, and you SURVIVED. Do you know how dope you are, girl? No matter what, you cannot change. You hear me?"

She nodded, sucking her bottom lip in between teeth as her nostrils flared and fresh tears came to her eyes. She looked down.

He cradled her face in his hands, forcing her to look at him. "Happy tears?" he whispered, his thumbs smoothing along her cheeks. "Hmm?"

Camryn was quiet, weeping silently as Bryson looked on, wiping her face, kissing her hands, squeezing her shoulders, and encouraging her to take her time. This was her moment to vent and to heal. Several minutes went by before she spoke again.

"I haven't had a good cry like that in awhile," she confessed, her head still downward and eyes puffy and lips pouty, and still looking absolutely stunning to him. "All this time, I've tried to be so brave and I've been so alone, and it's been tough...so to hear you say that...to *know* that someone is cheering for me and believes in me means everything. Thank you."

He smiled tenderly, not exactly sure what he was doing, but knowing it felt right. His eyes danced between her mouth and her eyes, taken aback by the beauty of both. She was emotional and he was emotional, but this made sense. It was something they had done when they were five-year-olds, hiding out under the double slides at recess. Heck, it was something he wanted to do when he first saw her at the dance, slipping through the crowd.

Bryson leaned forward and connected his lips with hers, gently and sweetly. She tasted even better than he imagined, her natural taste mixed in with salty tears and the lingering spearmint of her gum. Her mouth was smooth and though the kiss was feathery light, it held enough power to bring him to his knees. Thankfully, he was sitting.

Instinctively, his hand left her face and one trailed down her neck, while the other found the small of her back, urging her closer so that their chests were flush against each other. Bryson was well aware of their close proximity, the uncompromising position, the vulnerability of the situation, and the fact that they were still new to one another, but the kiss was the perfect encouragement and push in the right direction. Camryn needed assurance that she wasn't alone, and Bryson wanted to show her that she had *nothing* to fear. She could reveal herself to him— the *real* her.

The kiss ended when a soft groan sounded. It

was subtle yet distinct enough to be heard over the music. Bryson's eyes snapped open as their lips parted with a pop, their breaths heavy and staggered. She also opened her eyes and a sheepish look took over her features. Her lips were now swollen as she touched them shyly and then giggled.

"I'm sorry."

"What was that?" he chuckled.

"My stomach." She looked up at him under her long, dark eyelashes. "Can we grab my clothes and then go back…to my place? I can make us some coffee and French toast. That is, if you aren't ready to leave me."

He leaned a final time to hug her shortly and then kiss her forehead. "You had me at French toast."

CHAPTER 5

Camryn was being stupid.

No, no. She was being silly. Honestly, she was acting like a complete fool.

Really, she was walking around and giggling like a schoolgirl.

This...was...utterly...dumb.

But being stupid, silly, and dumb and acting like a foolish schoolgirl never felt so good. It had been a little more than two weeks since she and Bryson kissed and began regularly seeing each other. On school nights, he typically called and talked to her until they both fell asleep, and then on the weekends, it was usually a night out on Friday, breakfast on Saturday, a dinner date that same day, and then a home cooked meal the following Sunday. When Bryson wasn't working, he was stopping by the school to visit Junie in her classroom and then volunteering to help Camryn after school to straighten her room or simply sit and watch her work.

She tapped her fingers on the desk, remembering two nights ago when he did the most romantic thing she had ever experienced. He knew she had a couple teacher meetings and obligations, and had gotten the keys to her home while she finished up at school. He had setup a candlelight dinner that he orchestrated from the appetizer and entrée to the dessert and music choices. Rose petals had covered her kitchen table and he had waited on her hand and foot. Other than his slightly burned scalloped potatoes, she was quite impressed with his cooking and his courting. He knew exactly how to treat a woman and it showed in his actions and words.

She was lucky.

Seeing Bryson felt amazing, like the feeling of having new crisp bed sheets waiting for you after a long hard day's work. He was refreshing in every aspect and the total package. He had a good heart, good looks, and good intentions. But she was never one to fall head over heels for just the outward appearance. True, the beard, nice smile, and muscles for days were appreciated, but he also had substance. He was an outstanding father figure for his niece; he was great to talk to, and he seemed to want to make the world a better place.

She was thankful each day that God had brought them back together. He was the perfect friend and confidant...and good God Almighty, the things he could do with his lips and large hands, as he cupped her face, or massaged her lower back, or caressed her arms. Knowing there was someone else in her corner that she could lean on and trust was a downright Godsend, and while there was no title on what their relationship was, she liked the challenge and newness. When the time was right, it would be explored, but for now, she enjoyed the innocence of things.

"Miss Foster, can you help me log in? Miss Foster?"

Camryn's expression went from dreamy to surprised as she snapped herself back to reality. Thanksgiving Break was long gone and Christmas Break was over a week away, but not coming quickly enough. When that time came, she planned to sleep in as much as possible, enjoy watching home makeover shows, and cook her favorite meals for breakfast and dinner. She would also spend a majority of her nights kissing Bryson like they were love struck teenagers and watching cheesy Christmas movies until the wee hours of the mornings with him half asleep on her couch. The thought excited her.

But for now, she had an entire classroom of rambunctious children that deserved her attention and guidance. Dominique, the first grader who was calling her name at the top of his lungs, and the remainder of Room 3 needed to be supervised.

She giggled to herself, thinking about Bryson and how *he* needed supervision half the time whenever he came over. They could be watching a romantic comedy and he'd suddenly start tickling her, and somehow they would end up with his arm thrown over a shoulder, her face close to his, and his lips on hers. Or he would be whispering sweet nothings in her ear as his other hand played in her hair. Or she would find herself in his arms as he sang off-key, as loudly as he could, while they danced to a song in one of the movie scenes. She giggled again, sighing, and looking out of the window, thinking of him.

"Miss Foster, can you *pleeeeeease* help me?" Dominique whined again and she had to mentally chastise herself.

"Oh! I'm sorry, honey." She looked down at the frustrated little boy, his brown hair fisted in his hands, and his glasses hiked up as he scrunched his nose. She knelt down beside him. "What's your password?"

"I dunno. Thas why I need YO' help," he rationalized, his eyes almost watery and his diction youthful and untrained.

"Dominique, it's okay," she chuckled, removing his fingers from his hair and then rubbing his back. "If ever you can't remember your password, always think about your birthdate. Then put the year behind it. When's your birthday?"

He thought about it for a moment. "November third."

"Okay, great." She stood up and smoothed her dress around her hips and backside. "So your password is," she leaned around him, her arms enveloping his while she typed, "Eleven-zero-three…and what comes after, did we say? What year are we in?"

"Mmm. *2019?*" His eyes sparkled in anticipation.

"Yes! There you go, honey. Good job. Eleven-zero-three-two-zero-one-nine! That's your password. Try it."

She patted his shoulder and gave a sweet smile as his index finger punched in the remaining numbers. She couldn't help chuckling at the adorable way his tongue stuck out of the side of his mouth in concentration. When the computer was fully logged in, he turned and gave her a thumbs up, his blue shirt stained with the frozen strawberry Popsicle he'd devoured at lunch.

"Thank you, Miss Foster!"

"You're welcome, Dominique. Anybody else need help logging in?" Camryn asked, looking around but all she could hear was the low hum of the reading programs that the children were playing. "Remember, you should be on reading games only. I don't want to see any math games. We are reading *The Very Hungry Caterpillar* by Eric Carle, one of my FAVORITE stories as a child and even as an adult. Pay special attention to the foods that are mentioned and all the colorful pictures that the illustrator used. Once you finish that, move on to *If You Give a Mouse a Cookie* by Laura Numeroff. That's another one of my favorites. Complete the cookie assignment at the end and try to sound out some of the words in the glossary. Do we understand what's expected?"

A chorus of "Okays" and "Alrights" and "Yes, Miss Fosters" erupted. She spent the next few minutes walking through the rows of strategically placed round tables, helping students pronounce certain words, nodding to some of their observations, and then giving stern looks to a few of the children who had logged onto YouTube when they thought she wasn't looking.

By the time class was over, 20 of her 24 children had completed both stories and the connecting activities as she'd instructed them. The other four—all boys—were sitting, arms crossed defiantly, legs swinging with attitude, and their lips poked out from Missouri to California. They had been pulled off for repeatedly doing the wrong thing and had been reprimanded accordingly. If they were any older, she would have had them write *I Will Follow Directions* on line paper 100 times, like she and many other classmates had to do back in the 90s.

The workday was fairly smooth. Besides the four classes she had, Principal Schumacher had also assigned her to do two lunch duties after two other faculty members called in sick to work. She successfully made it out of the cafeteria with only a single ketchup handprint to the side of her dress, thanks to one of the second graders who *insisted* she needed a hug.

Then, by 3:30pm, Camryn was practically bursting out of the double doors, ready to release her feet from their high heel prison and pull her hair up that was tickling her neck. She strolled out to the parking lot, her eyes trained on the candy apple red sedan she drove and had nearly tucked her hand under the handle to pull it open when she felt a hand at her waist and saw another arm reach around to keep her door from closing. She gave a high-pitched scream into the crisp afternoon, her eyes wide and her mouth even wider. There was no one in the immediate vicinity, so she fell into survival mode. She was thankful for the self-defense classes she'd taken and the *Lifetime* movies she'd watched over the years. Somebody was getting hurt today.

With as much strength as she could muster, her elbows went back and slammed into the perpetrator. She could hear someone—a man— grunt and then fall while she reached into the front flap of her workbag and retrieved a bottle of pepper spray that she was hoping she would never have to use. Camryn whipped around, her shawl briefly blowing up in the breeze and blinding her, but she aimed anyway, just barely missing the man's full face and only dousing his left eye as he moved on the ground pitifully, helplessly.

She stepped back a few paces, her backside slamming into the side of her car as she fought to get away while also getting a good look at the man through the red haze of mace. There was something familiar about his large hands and broad shoulders, and even his sense of style. She looked over the now crumpled, tailored suit jacket, and the cufflink initials that read *NR*, as the man struggled to sit up on his knees and cover his lone, burning eye. He moaned louder, demanding her to calm down, and his normally low voice was much higher in agonizing pain. Wait, it couldn't be. She knew him for the jokester he was. Regret and guilt washed over her as she dropped everything and knelt beside him.

"Mr. Rubio? What are you...? How did you...?"

"Miss Foster, please," he begged, tears coating his rounded face. He was red-faced and flushed. "Don't touch anything! Just...just let me figure this out for a second. Ugh! My EYE!" he complained.

She chewed nervously on her lower lip, looking at Nash Rubio, one of the board of directors for the school district and the man who had placed her at Elm Grove Elementary many years ago. His clothes were now dirty from rolling around on the ground, and his pea coat had fallen from his arms, she assumed, when her elbows had socked him. He looked desperate for relief of the peppery mix, unable to open his one eye, and crying thick tears from the other one. There was even a reddish-orangey mist near the collar of his dress shirt where the mace had landed. God, she hoped she wasn't going to lose her job.

It took more than an hour for the pepper spray residue to be semi-cleaned and washed from Mr. Rubio's eyes and face. He was able to retrieve cartons of leftover milk from the cafeteria and went into one of the gym showers to wash his eyes out with the milk, warm water, and an antibacterial soap that the school nurse provided. By the time he emerged, toweled off, and redressed, his face was still a bright red, but at least he was no longer crying and the burning sensation had lessened significantly.

Camryn felt even worse when she bade him goodbye and saw his ruined clothes and heard the scratchiness in his throat. He would have to go home and explain to his wife the scenario, and it wouldn't be fun. He made it known that he wasn't upset with her, though. He realized grabbing her around the waist wasn't exactly the right way to get her attention, but apparently, he'd called her several times and she had not heard him.

Mr. Rubio had only dropped by to tell her she would be getting a raise and to congratulate her on helping bring up the school's overall reading scores. She was given an ugly mug with an apple on it, to add to the other three she'd gotten in previous years, and a star pin. As she finally climbed into her car, Camryn couldn't help but to rub her own eyes with the heels of her palms and let out a fatigued sigh. That exhale turned into a disbelieving chuckle, and then finally a yawn, as she pulled off from the nearly vacant parking lot and headed home.

She was so exhausted, she sent Bryson a goodnight text as she warmed up leftovers, showered, and then climbed into bed.

Hopefully, tomorrow's workday ended drastically different.

"Hey, lady, how are you? What're your plans this evening?"

Camryn looked towards the doorway over the

brim of her coffee mug, filled to capacity with a French vanilla roast, and a dancing fog of steam that nearly singed her nose and upper lip each time she took a sip. She swallowed, winced at the heat trickling down her throat, and then answered.

"I didn't have any as of yet."

She looked over at the third grade teacher, who was leaning in and looked every bit of 30, but was pushing 50. In fact, this weekend was her 48th birthday, and yet, there she stood in black high-waisted pants, a sleeveless white blouse, sky-high stilettos, and a super cute chunky belt that matched the blood red jacket and purse she'd strolled in with. This probably was the reason for her impromptu visit between lunch hours.

Normally, Camryn didn't really socialize with her coworkers other than the typical conversations like "Hi, bye, how was your weekends." Lately, thanks to Bryson, she had been opening up more and *living* more. She had been allowing people to finally get to know *her*. That included heading to lunch with fellow grade level teachers, attending the secretary's baby shower at a local pavilion, and accepting an invite to an all-staff member baseball game.

Baby steps.

Miss Gilbert stepped further inside of the library, rubbing her damp hands on a brown napkin, and looking around for any straggling students. When she didn't see any, she dropped her professionalism. "I had a few extra minutes before I have to grab my kiddos. Thought I'd stop by and see what you were up to, and invite you for dinner tonight as I celebrate another year of getting older."

Camryn eyed the woman skeptically, watching her toss the napkin in a trashcan. If she recalled correctly, she had an important late movie date with a certain six-foot, sexy, brown-eyed fella by the name of Bryson. If she played her cards right, she could make both engagements. "Where? What time? I'll have to double-check my schedule, but I'd love to join you if I can."

"Have you ever been to the *Sip & Sip Café* on Third? Some of the ladies are meeting there early at six for dinner, or you can join us for the painting part at seven. Should be fun."

The *Sip & Sip Café* was a popular downtown restaurant that specialized in all sorts of wines and soups, and its painters were some of Missouri's premier artists from what Camryn had heard.

"That sounds fun," Camryn admitted, placing the cap over the tip of her blue ink pen. "I'm down."

"Good! I was hoping you would be." Miss Gilbert winked, her green eyes sparkling with mischief. She leaned a hip onto the desk, and crossed her legs at the ankles. "Are you familiar with the inspiration behind the canvases they paint?"

Camryn's eyes rolled upward in thought. "Mmm. No, not really. Why?" Camryn didn't miss the way the middle-aged woman lit up, her lips curving into a wide smile.

"Well, honey, you're in for a TREAT then! Leave all your inhibitions at home and come with an open mind."

"I'm not sure I like the sound of that," Camryn admitted and giggled.

Miss Gilbert pushed off of the desk and checked her slim wristwatch. "No, no, trust me, it'll be fun. And you're welcome to head down the block with us to Euphoria and get a couple *stronger* drinks and do a little dancing afterward, but I know you aren't a big drinker or party girl, so no pressure."

"Yeah, I'll have to let you know for sure, okay?"

"Sounds good!" Miss Gilbert sauntered out with her hands tucked in her pockets, and then peeked back over a shoulder abruptly, her brown hair whipping around her. "Oh, and remind me to give you my number later. Have a good rest of your day."

"Yeah, you too!" Camryn gave a quick nod and smile.

Hours later, Camryn was home and resting her feet before she had to get dolled up all over again for ladies' night with her coworkers. Never in a million years would she have imagined letting her guard completely down and accepting an invite out to the busiest part of town without any hesitation.

Because she was not accustomed to going out, even on special occasions, she had no appropriate ladies' night outfit lying around in her closet. She definitely didn't want to look like a schoolteacher in her conservative hues and calf-length skirts, and had stopped by the department store to shop and treat herself with a few essentials—two little black dresses, fitting jeans, and even a new lingerie set that no one would probably see until her wedding night, but it was empowering to purchase nonetheless.

She was proud of herself and kept a smile on her face while she pulled on her new long-sleeved black dress that skimmed the tops of her knees and comfortable, black, thigh-high leather boots that she bought online the year before. It was probably not the wisest, considering she planned on painting, but the material of the garment felt and looked amazing against her skin. She put on a bright lip to give her a splash of color, and imagined Bryson seeing her in a few more hours. Surely he'd make some flirty remark about the length of her dress, the smell of her hair, or the way the lipstick accented her mouth. The thought made her smile as she texted him a hello, and then gathered a small handbag.

By the time she was bustling through the house and turning off the final few lights, Miss Gilbert was honking the horn outside. To add onto her day of newness and adventure, Camryn had actually allowed the women to know where she lived. Progress.

"Hey, Skylar. Looking good in that dress, girl. I knew you had a body up under those school clothes," a voice called out from the back. It was one of the fifth grade teaching assistants. Alongside her were two other unfamiliar women, all sporting warm smiles and kind eyes.

Camryn paused as she climbed into the passenger seat of Miss Gilbert's truck. The only problem with enjoying this new life of freedom is she would have to get comfortable with answering to two different names. Everyone knew her as Skylar Foster still, and probably always would, for her safety. It was Bryson who had gotten her familiarized with her former identity.

"Thank you, Mrs. Chalmers."

"I am not Mrs. Chalmers tonight, girlfriend. My momma named me Sylvia, and I demand that you call me that. This is also my cousin, Cheri, and her friend, Olive."

Camryn did a round of "hey, how you doings" at the women and smiled. She was ready to have a good time with like-minded ladies, if only for a few hours.

CHAPTER 6

Following her hilarious and eventful ladies' night of painting canvases and admiring half naked male models, and then laughing it up over dinner and virgin drinks, Camryn was dropped back off at home. The women begged her to partake in a little dancing, but she emphasized her date later that evening with Bryson and bailed, promising that tonight wouldn't be her last night of spending time with them outside of school. She waved a final goodbye to her colleagues and watched them pull off.

When she turned back around, she was startled to find a small, huddled figure near her doorstep. She paused in her forward motion, turning on the light from her cell phone so that she could get a good look at who or what was waiting for her. She saw shivering shoulders, bent knees, chipped nail polish on tiny hands covering a rounded face and then finally, eyes peering over those short hands. It couldn't be…no, it couldn't be…*Junie?*

Camryn quickened her movements, alarmed for the troubled little girl. What in the world? This was the second time Junie had come to her for safety. "Junie, what's the matter? How you'd get here? Where's your coat? What—what happened, honey?"

She realized quickly that her million and one questions probably wasn't calming the little girl, so she gathered her in her arms and opened the front door. She rushed inside, Junie slightly slipping in her arms, as she flicked on lights and turned up the thermostat in her house. Junie's skin was cold and pale, a far cry from her normally golden brown skin and Camryn had to wonder how long the child had been outside.

"Come sit down by the fireplace. Are you hungry?"

Junie nodded, her nose running and her eyes

glassy. Camryn handed her a handful of tissue and was never gladder that she had cooked a big pot of chili the night before as she heated some up on the stove and then went to retrieve a thick blanket from her guest bedroom.

As she tucked the comforter around Junie's frame, she patted her body for her phone. She briefly remembered leaving it outside and slipped into her house shoes, retrieving her purse that still lay on the concrete, and locking back up. She had to wonder if it was the same issue with Junie's mother, as she called Bryson. He didn't answer her on the first, second, or third call, so she left a message, keeping her voice as calm as possible for both Bryson's sanity and Junie's listening ears.

"Hey, it's Cam. Can you please stop by my house when you can? I know we were planning to get together later, but I need you *now*. I, um, have your niece here. Thanks."

It was nearly two hours later that Bryson's frantic knock sounded at the door as the nine o'clock hour approached. At least she assumed it was him, because there was no call or text message, and no one else knew where she lived besides the few women she worked with. She looked over at Junie who was still cocooned in a warm blanket, a half-cup of hot chocolate in her hands, and an amused grin on her face as they watched a Christmas comedy.

Prior to sitting down with the chili and marshmallow-filled hot chocolate, Camryn had given Junie a bath and then changed her into one of her oversized lounge shirts and shorts that were baggy but warm. Camryn had also washed the little girl's hair, and brushed it back into a ponytail, noting the heaviness of the grease and dandruff throughout her matted locks. It had to have been several weeks since her last wash. Then, taking a speedy shower herself, she joined Junie and avoided the topic at hand. Wrapping a robe around her body and tying the drawstrings loosely around her hips, she snatched the heavy door open.

The one time Bryson decided to leave his phone on the charger while he worked out was the one time he was needed for an emergency. He was fresh out of the shower, his slim waist wrapped in a thick charcoal grey towel, and water dripping everywhere else, when he finally retrieved his phone. Four missed calls. Two voicemail messages. One urgent text message in all capital letters saying: *CALL ME ASAP— RE:JUNIE.* All from Camryn regarding his Junebug.

He really hadn't processed what was going on and didn't even bother contacting Junie's mother. Somehow he knew that beyond his nerves was the itch to be angry, and Briana would likely further upset him. Dressing speedily, he was on the highway within minutes and dared anybody in law enforcement to try and stop him. His mom would have had a fit with his actions—running outside in the cold, especially "with his pores open" from the warm shower he had just stepped out of, but logistics were out of the door. Junie needed him.

Bryson made it across town in record time, pulling in dangerously close to Camryn's garage door and slamming on brakes with a *skkrt*! He raced up to the front door, almost stumbling to the ground from his loosely tied boots, and banged with the sides of his balled fists. The sky was dark; the air was crisp, and he regretted not simply ringing the doorbell, as he noticed how several lights in the neighboring houses came on. It couldn't look good, a man half dressed with a bare chest peeking through an unzipped jacket, sweatpants hanging low on his hips, and boots practically falling from his large feet as he trudged to the window, unable to peek in because of the closed blinds and curtains.

"Cam! It's me," he added for good measure when he heard movement inside. He walked back to the front door to wait, tensing his shoulders up to his ears and rocking back and forth to keep warm.

Suddenly, he was exposed to the warmth of the house and a shocked set of knowing hazel-brown eyes. His gaze took Camryn in and his racing heart calmed instantly. She didn't look too worried, so he knew he had nothing to be worried about. Junie was safe; he could hear her giggles from where he stood.

"Hey," he breathed.

"Hey." She gave a small smile, reaching out to touch his arm.

"This is the best part, Miss Foster. Come back. You're missin' it!" she exclaimed at that moment.

They both smiled at her words, Bryson stepping inside with a sigh and Camryn locking up behind him.

When she turned back around, he couldn't help but look her over, once and then twice. She was sporting a cute red and black-checkered pajama set and her famous fuzzy socks that she seemed to wear each time he saw her. Maybe she had several pair. Yeah. That had to be it, because this pair had black and white polka dots, unlike the green and grey ones he saw before.

Her hair was glistening with moisture and smelled like honey and Shea butter, if his memory of scents served him correctly. Around her short frame was a cozy looking robe that clung to the swell of her hips and stopped mid-thigh on her. She was makeup-free, and without any jewelry, and looking absolutely comfortable in her skin— in *her* home.

He liked her most this way.

Bryson caught himself staring and forced his eyes past her shoulders, nodding to Junie. "So what happened? Thanks for calling me. I'm sorry I got your messages late. I was working out before our date later, and..."

He didn't miss the way her eyes followed the column of his neck and down his exposed chest and torso. She cleared her throat as he stood up a little straighter.

"Excuse my um...lack of clothes. I was showering, and kind of just...headed over." He smiled, feeling the need to explain. "I was worried," he added sheepishly.

"Well, you can't fit any of my clothes, so I'll get you a blanket or something. It's too cold outside to be half naked," she teased.

He could only muster up a slight smile at her words, his eyes still troubled. She noticed and grew serious.

"I found her huddled outside of my house and brought her in. I didn't ask her what was wrong. I felt like that was your place, but I did feed and bathe her, and washed and dried her school uniform." Camryn's voice lowered, "She had another accident."

He shook his head thoughtfully. "I didn't know she knew you lived here?"

"I didn't either. I have no idea how she found me, Bryson."

He followed behind her into the living room, with concern in his voice. "Junebug," he called. "What's going on, baby girl? You were supposed to get on the bus right after school, remember?"

She looked startled like she hadn't known he was there and then curled up a little tighter in the mound of pillows and blankets. "Hi, Uncle B," she barely whispered.

He leaned down to kiss her forehead, brushing his fingers through her semi-damp, wavy hair. "What happened today, baby girl?"

Camryn stepped forward, placing a hand on his arm. "Can I speak to you in the other room?"

He reluctantly tore his eyes away from his withdrawn niece and nodded to Camryn's soft words. "We'll be right back, okay, Junebug?" he called over a shoulder.

She nodded, her eyebrows knitting together as she lowered her eyes to the pillow she rested on.

Camryn led him to the laundry room where he could see a load jostling about in the massive machine. She had gotten it repaired a week ago. The dryer was also spinning rhythmically in time. Junie's clothes were neatly hanging up, clean and fragranced with fabric softener, and steamed to perfection. She pushed the door closed.

"I wasn't sure if I should bring this up, because I never want to assume the worst. But I've noticed at school and even earlier when I found her outside how she has accidents. Of course, it's normal for it to happen to a child every blue moon at this age, but it's happening pretty often. She visits my room at least once a week," she explained and then pressed her lips together in anticipation, studying his face.

Bryson nodded, following but not following. He shifted his weight from one foot to another uncomfortably. "You think she has like a female issue down there, or…?"

She motioned with her hands as she spoke slowly, *"Possibly*. A urinary tract infection, or a yeast infection, or...and I'm not trying to upset you, but sometimes little girls have accidents when they've...um...been exposed to...you know." Her hand hovered over her private parts for emphasis.

He continued to blink sluggishly, his mouth going dry and his pulse quickening as she continued hesitantly.

"I also checked her arms as I was drying her off. She has quite a few bruises, and—*Bryson?*"

He tuned her out. Her words were a blur, along with her concerned face, and her sweet touch to his hand. It wasn't his intention but he jerked away violently from her and he couldn't do anything to stop the bile from rising in his throat. His eyes clamped shut and he stumbled back into the wall as though he had been forcefully shoved. His knees suddenly felt weak and his mind wandered down a path he wasn't so sure he wanted it to go for the sake of everyone's safety.

"No, no. Camryn, no." His voice was husky

and thick with emotion. "You're not saying what I think you're saying. Don't—don't tell me that."

Bryson slid down the wall, blinding anger pricking his heart, confusion clouding his mind, and tears of helplessness gathering to fill his dark eyes. With just a few words, his world had come crashing down.

"Cam, what are you thinking? You're saying she was...*raped?*" The word caused him to choke.

"Please listen. Don't get worked up. I—I don't know for sure and I can't make assumptions." She dropped down beside him onto her knees, planting her hands on his bent legs. "I want nothing more than to tell you no, but I wanted you to know firsthand what *I* have noticed."

His head rocked left to right, back and forth. His hope was that the more he shook his head, the quicker the thoughts and ideas and anger would subside.

"Has there ever been any concerns about this in the past? I know her mother has a boyfriend around."

The dams broke. His restraint broke. All hell broke loose. "Camryn, that's a child!" he cried out, his words shaky. "Junie is SIX YEARS OLD!"

She flinched, moving closer to sit beside him. "Shhh. I know, I know. Calm down. I just want to help you figure this thing out."

He relaxed completely against the wall, thankful he had something to hold him up and support him. He was quiet as he thought of all the years of looking after Junie, the years of being in her life and being the father figure she needed, the years of promising to love, provide for, and protect her. Usually he was there, front and center, and on the battlefield for her. Only he hadn't protected her this time, and he had a serious problem with that.

"I'm going to kill Ashton," he threatened, referring to his sister-in-law's boyfriend.

Abruptly, he used the wall and the strength in his legs to slide up into a stand. In the process, Camryn was knocked back slightly, and fell back onto her palms. If he weren't so heated, he would have helped her to a stand and apologized, but all he could focus on was destroying the strange man that Briana kept cooped in her home. His eyes seemed to darken to black and became squinted pools of fury, and his upper body tensed almost painfully while he stepped towards the door.

"I'm going to KILL HIM!" he yelled again, suddenly punching the wall behind him.

Camryn rushed to her feet and shushed to quiet him, placing her hands on his tense shoulders, and backing him away from the door. "Wait, wait! Bryson, calm down. Look at me! Please wait and think this through. We have to ask questions first and then throw out accusations later!"

"I need to find him and talk to him. Let me go, Camryn."

"To go where? No, you're staying HERE! Don't you DARE leave my house without speaking to her and figuring this out first. I'd hate for you to get thrown in jail over a misunderstanding."

As far as Bryson was concerned, her words were null and void as he saw red. His eyes blurred with unshed tears and his body warmed involuntarily from his head to his feet. "He hurt her! The signs are all there. How could I have missed that? Let me go, Camryn. I'm not trying to hurt you or be disrespectful, so please step aside and let me go," he pleaded, his voice low with rage.

"I'm not letting you go, especially when you're looking and acting like this."

"HE...HURT...HER!" Bryson yelled loud enough for probably Junie to hear but at that point, no one but God Himself could stop him.

"But do we really know that? I was only making an observation because I've seen it a couple times before in different cases with the children I work with, Bryson. I've also experienced sexual abuse personally, and those were some of the things I dealt with, but we don't know for sure. Are you listening? *Bryson*. Look at me. No, *LOOK* at me. Please hear me out."

Her petite fingers caressed his jawline, forcing his face in the direction of hers. As much as he didn't want to listen, he gave her that much respect and attention. Reluctantly, his gaze peered down at her, a single tear falling leisurely from his furious, troubled eyes. His breaths left his nostrils in spurts, fanning out over her face. Bryson could feel his heart pumping erratically, echoing in his ears. *Ka-thump. Ka-thump. Ka-thump.*

When he spoke, he hardly recognized his voice. "You don't understand. This is beyond reasoning. He took it too far. I...promised to protect her and I didn't. Now she's scared to go home!"

"I KNOW that! But you have to calm down!"

"I ain't calming down!" He attempted to shrug her off of him. "Let me go, Camryn!"

"Listen to me," she begged, placing a cautious hand to his bicep while the other nestled against his chest. "This was beyond your control. You had no idea that there could be something going on at home, and you still don't because you haven't sat down and asked. She needs you to be her strength right now; she needs you to be her uncle right now. Not her hero. If you leave out of this door and go and do something crazy, and get locked up or WORSE, not only will Junie lose you, but...but..."

Bryson focused on the wall behind her head, doing his best to ignore the tears forming in her eyes.

"...I'd lose you too. And call me selfish," she

added softly, cupping her hands along his jawline and tenderly holding his face inches from hers, "but I can't have that. I...I can't lose you. Junie can't lose you. You're all we have. You're all *I* have."

He was stunned by her words, so honest and filled with emotions. Finally, he faced her completely and took a moment to breathe and steady his breathing. The look in her eyes shook his core, and as much as he hated to admit it, she was right. He could leave her house, play big guy, and do as much damage as he wanted, but where would that leave him? Where would that leave *them,* and their budding relationship? He was too accomplished and had too much responsibility to go down that path. If anybody deserved a mug shot, it wasn't him. It was Ashton.

She pulled him into a hug and held him there, occasionally standing on tiptoes to kiss his temple and his lips, rub his back, and rock their bodies. It took another fifteen minutes for his breathing to return to normal, for both of their tears to stop, and for Camryn to allow him to leave her arms and sidestep her.

"Can we talk to her now? I just—I have to know. I promise I won't do anything else."

"I know you're anxious about this, but it's late. She's tired. Just sleep on it and let's try to sit down tomorrow with a clear head."

"She's not going to school tomorrow, I can tell you that. I'll just call Briana tomorrow and tell her Junie's staying with me from now on, if she even cares."

"That's fine. Sure." Camryn nodded, walking alongside him towards the living room.

The TV still blared, the fireplace still flickered, but the lone occupant on the couch was now peacefully sleeping. Bryson's eyes immediately were drawn to his niece. She was curled up on her side, with her hands folded under her cheek, and her lips pouty and slightly parted. He walked over, kneeled down to kiss her forehead, and then brushed his thick fingertips across her hairline, along the span of her dark hair, over her flushed cheek, and then finally smoothed down her arm. With a whispered, *"Sweet dreams, baby girl,"* he tucked her in a little tighter and then turned the TV off.

When he looked up, Camryn was watching him with misty eyes. He offered a small smile, joining her in the kitchen. "I know this is a big request, but can you please let her stay with you tonight? She's sleeping well, and I'd hate to move her around or drive with her across town at this hour."

She was nodding before he even finished. "I've already decided to call in. She can spend the day with me while you do whatever it is that you need to do to make sure Briana and Ashton are reported. You can even put my name on the complaints because I'm a mandated reporter, you know, being part of the school staff and all. You can say I brought it to your attention and you took the necessary steps to investigate. I don't care what we have to do. Just make sure she's taken care of, as you always do," she spoke reassuringly.

He studied her, standing there and speaking to him with such assurance and compassion, and felt a strange chill run throughout his veins. His heart fluttered as he thought of the measures she had taken to ensure *his* niece was okay. He was blown away by the way she was able to calm Junie down and care for her, and then calm *him* down in his moment of weakness, and still keep a level head through it all. When they reunited, she didn't ask for the extra baggage, especially with all that she was juggling with, in her personal life. She didn't have to go beyond the duty of being a teacher and stepping in the way she was doing, but she had done it with grace and zero hesitation, and it meant the world to him.

"Camryn—I..."

She cut him off with a knowing smile. "I know, Bryson. I already know and understand what you're going to say. I would have done it even if she weren't my student, or your niece. She deserves to be happy, healthy, and safe—everyone does. You don't have to thank me."

"At least let me thank you for talking me off of the ledge. I could've ruined a lot for us tonight."

Camryn simply took him by the hands and pulled him closer. She embraced him for a second time, running her hands up his chest and over the curve of his shoulders where she massaged them. "*Shhhh,*" she coaxed. "Free your mind, baby. Let's discuss something else for the moment. My day was productive and long. I went out with some of the ladies from work."

"Did you? Thatta girl. You have fun? Where did you go?" he mumbled, licking his lips and allowing her to discard his jacket and then pull him further down one of the carpeted hallways. He assumed she was leading him to a guestroom. "Proud of you, Cam..."

She kept her eyes on his as she walked backward, recalling her time out and turning off lights as she went. "I'm very proud of myself too.

We painted. We ate a little dinner. *They* drank wine. I was invited to some dancing, but I knew you and I had a date."

He frowned for a moment, suddenly aware of their interrupted plans for the evening. "I'm sorry all of this took place and got in our way."

She cocked her head to the side. "Ah, ah, ah. What did I say? We're not going to dwell on what did and did not happen. Besides, me and Junie had a good time watching movies and eating and chatting like old friends. Now, you and I are going to enjoy a little dancing that you promised me and then head to bed. Yes, you're staying the night. You can take one of these guestrooms we just passed by."

"Where are we headed now, pretty lady?" He reached out to run his fingers along her smooth skin, fighting back a smile.

"The queen's palace," she teased, pulling him into her massive bedroom where he got a glimpse of her resting place for the first time.

It was feminine with warm shades of lavender and lilac, and styled as he imagined it would be. Sheer canopy curtains were draped over her extra high bed frame; fuzzy rugs were nestled over certain spots of the hardwood floor; artwork featuring flowers, beaches and dramatic sunsets hung throughout the room; a walk-in closet was only slightly visible from his position by the door; a small couch was stationed at the foot of the bed, and a vanity with everything a woman could ever need sat off to the side of her single book shelf and entertainment center.

"Wow."

She followed his eyes around the room. "This is where the magic happens. Isn't that what people say on those TV shows when they show off their homes?" she laughed.

"What magic?" He lifted an eyebrow playfully. "There better not be any magic going on."

"Sleeping, of course." She winked and shrugged off her robe, sauntering over to her closet. "Like I said, I don't have any clothes that you can fit, but you're welcome to one of these sweatshirts that the school gave me that were too big."

Bryson watched her in disbelief. "Woman, I am *not* wearing your clothes. I'm fine for the night in this."

"You sure? I tend to keep a cold house since it's just me."

"I'll be fine."

"Okay, handsome. Whateva you say," she sang, closing in on him. He barely registered what she was saying before she claimed his mouth for a second time.

"So about this dancing," he mumbled against her lips, as soft as cotton and sweet to the taste. He could make out traces of hot chocolate and marshmallows on her tongue. "Mmmm."

"Mmmhmm. Shhh." She kissed him for a moment, never breaking contact as their arms entangled and she blindly walked them to the balcony. His eyes opened slightly, catching the beautiful deck beyond the glass doors, hammock, frozen pond, and trees. He would have to enjoy the home's beauty in the daylight, or whenever she released him. He really didn't want that second option though.

"You smell good," she whispered.

"You make me feel good," he countered, the seriousness of his words causing her head to lift abruptly. "You are really something special, you know that?"

"You've mentioned it before." She smiled shyly, swaying back and forth.

"I'll mention it again and again until you realize it. Thank you for everything. Thank you for being you, Cam. It's been a pleasure getting to know you better over this last month. I'm happy God led us back together."

"You've been an answered prayer for me too," she confessed. Her forehead crinkled in concentration while she worked on rubbing traces of her lipstick off of his lips. Up until now, he hadn't noticed the faint traces of it on her pouty mouth.

"Oh yeah?"

"Mmhmm."

He smiled. "You know...Every year, I run down this Christmas wish list for me and Junie. She understands the real meaning of Christmas; she recognizes it's Jesus's birthday, and how she should be grateful beyond receiving gifts, but I still let her believe in Santa, leave out cookies, and write out her lists and the whole nine. This year, her number one wish was for you to join us for Christmas."

He was sure that if he could see her heart from the inside out, it would have fluttered. She smiled leisurely, her eyes watering ever so slightly. "Join you for Christmas, how? For dinner?"

"I guess so. Except I have one dilemma." He held up his index finger for emphasis.

Camryn cocked her head to the side in question.

"We won't be in St. Louis for the holidays, even though she doesn't know that. I'm surprising her with a trip to Disney World."

"And why's that a dilemma? Disney is so fun and exciting. At least that's what I've gathered from a few colleagues that went as children."

Bryson smiled. "The problem is, she wants YOU to join US for Christmas. She believes in Santa and if Santa doesn't honor her number one wish, the poor girl's heart may break. We can't have that."

"Soooo...you're saying?" Camyrn could not stop smiling and blushing, not quite understanding, but smitten by his words.

Bryson realized he'd have to work for his next words.

"I'm saying, Miss Camryn Young, we have an entire suite and plenty of room for you to join us. That is, if you'd like. All I'd have to do is get you a plane ticket and boom! My wish...I mean, *Junie's wish* has come true." His hands kneaded into the small of her back while he held her. "So what do you say?"

Camryn couldn't help but to grin widely at his sweet and nervous proposition. She thought it over, tapping her finger against the side of her mouth and rolling her eyes upward. She stepped back. "Mmmm. I'll have to check my schedule and then ask my boyfriend. You know, see if he approves this little getaway you seemed to have planned."

"Your boyfriend, huh?" He chuckled and pulled her against him roughly yet playfully again, and then dipped his head in the column of her neck. He mumbled, "Tell whoever he is to kick rocks. He missed out on his chance."

Camryn giggled when he proceeded to tickle her with light kisses up and down her neck and the side of her face. He knew those certain spots that made her blush and enjoyed taking advantage of her weaknesses. "Yeaaah, you're right. I'd much rather have you anyway."

An hour later, Bryson was closing the guest bedroom door shut and practically dancing across the floor to turn down the goose feather duvet. He slipped inside the bed and yawned loudly unintentionally, his lips still swollen from kissing Camryn. If he closed his eyes hard enough, he could still feel her in his arms, soft and womanly and deliciously warm. He could certainly still smell her, from her hair, and natural scent, to the lotion she'd likely smoothed on after her shower.

He was excited that she'd agree to go to

Florida with them and hoped nothing changed her mind. The ticket had already been purchased, so if she hadn't agreed, he would have been out of a few hundred bucks. He planned on showing her a good time and finally telling her the things he knew were much too early to be said but that she deserved to hear. The truth was, he was falling and falling quickly for her hypnotizing eyes, relentless compassion, and intoxicating smile.

More and more, he was thinking of her every day, and constantly wondering how he could make her life better. He enjoyed watching her eyes light up whenever they spent time together, and he even appreciated her always laughing at his jokes even when they weren't all that funny. The way she treated Junie was even more amazing and attractive. She seemed to love his niece as if she were family too, and he couldn't get over how naturally nurturing she was. Camryn was wife and mother material, for sure.

As he stretched out even further, his joints crackled. He rested a hand across his torso and sighed, looking up towards the ceiling. His mind left the euphoria that was Camryn, and involuntarily raced back to the issue at hand and the reason he was even staying over in the first place. This was not the news he was expecting or ever wanted to hear, and he was determined to get to the bottom of Junie's bruises, runaway spells, and frequent accidents.

He planned to not only schedule a doctor's appointment to make sure there were no scars or injuries to her private parts, but he also wanted to have a good talk with her when she was ready to speak up and tell her secrets. For now, as hard as it was, he wouldn't push or pressure her.

As much as he didn't want to fall asleep for fear that he would miss out on something else, sleep claimed him and silenced his thoughts and gave him much more peace than he thought possible.

CHAPTER 7

Two weeks later...

I t was the morning before Christmas and the morning of their Disney getaway, and of all days, the morning Bryson decided to have a one-on-one with Briana and Ashton. He'd left Junie with Camryn, who graciously offered to watch the little girl and help her pack up any remaining belongings that were tucked in the closets and drawers of his apartment.

He was across town, practically sitting shoulder-to-shoulder with a half-sleeping Briana, and Ashton across the room in a worn recliner, glaring at him. He ignored the man's beady eyes, and then turned the TV off, seeing how it was distracting Briana. He openly stared at her until she finally caught his eyes. She wrapped her arms around herself, warding off the chill of the rundown home, clad in a cotton housecoat, slippers, and plastic hair rollers.

"I'm going to keep this short and simple because I have a plane to catch. I'm not assuming you put your hands on my niece. I'm just going off what I see and what she and the doctor told me," Bryson finally spoke, his hands clasped and his tone even and low.

Junie had opened up reluctantly about the bruises on her body and why she couldn't hold her bladder. Apparently, Briana and Ashton had gotten rough with each other one night. Junie had stepped in to try to break the scuffle up, was much too small, and all three of them had fallen into a heap on the floor when they were suddenly thrown off balance by her tugging. As for her accidents, she was often awakened at night to screams and gunshots in their neighborhood, which haunted her.

The doctors had also thoroughly checked her

out and made sure she was free of any yeast or urinary tract infections, and any injuries sustained by abuse. Those findings backed up Junie's claims. She promised her uncle that no man or boy, or woman, for that matter, had touched her "private parts." The night that she'd shown up to Camryn's house was the night of the fight and she knew where Camryn lived because of all the rides she'd taken with Bryson. Plus, "you can see the top of her house from school!" she'd exclaimed.

All was well in the sense that Bryson wouldn't have to go to jail over pummeling the man's head in, but he was still uneasy over their living arrangements. He wanted Junie under his care full-time and wasn't going to stop pursuing it until that happened.

"I didn't touch anybody!" Ashton exclaimed, already slurring at nine o'clock in the morning and probably filled with some dark liquor.

"Nobody except Briana, right? Junie told me everything. She told me about your fights, your tantrums, and your arguments. She's not coming back after this trip. I'm taking her with me to live until you can get yourself together."

"Says *who*?!" Ashton croaked.

"Says the man who takes care of her 99 percent of the time! Says the man who isn't introducing her to violence, sleepless nights, and instilling fear in her!" Bryson raised his voice. "Why are you even talking? You're not her father or stepfather, or any kin to this family! You're just shackin' up!"

"You can't take my child from me," Briana said weakly, sitting upright to try to regain some sense of control in the room.

"The courts would say otherwise. Get yourself together, get rid of this 160-pound USELESS man that does nothing but stress you out, and get back to the Briana my brother married! Bryant treated you like a queen and then you settle with—with somebody like *Ashton*? You gotta clean yourself up before you destroy your life, Bri. I'm not saying this to tear you down, but because I love you."

She shoved a finger in Bryson's chest, her eyes finally coming alive and burning with anger. He was at least happy to see some sort of reaction and emotion from her otherwise lifeless demeanor. "You don't understand the pain I felt after losing your brother! You don't comprehend the pain I STILL FEEL! It's hard to carry on and be a good mother. Who are you to judge me? I do the best I can for Junie and you know it."

"I'm not judging you, but I am laying out all the facts. You're *not* doing the best you can otherwise you wouldn't be spending your money on drugs and cigarettes and liquor. You need help and until you receive it, I'm going to remove Junie from this situation. You and I both know she's better off with me. Your best—I'm sorry to say— is not good enough. And don't you dare tell me you're hurting more over Bryant. You were his wife of six years, I get it. But I was his brother for over 22 years. That man was my lifeline and my best friend. I know it hurts but you don't see me resorting to drugs and neglecting my responsibilities. Yes, it hurts, but life goes on! Life doesn't stop, especially when you have a child who needs you and who's relying on you! Don't give me that!" he yelled, standing to his feet. He'd had enough, plus the pungent smell of stale liquor, traces of marijuana, and dirty laundry was beginning to make him nauseous.

Ashton also stood, trying his best to stay upright and look intimidating. Bryson looked him over, chuckled bitterly, and then shook his head. "What are you tryin' to do?"

"Get outta my house!" the man hissed and pointed. "Now look, you're getting her all upset."

"*Your* house, huh? You're not paying any bills, so you have no right to say something is yours." Bryson held up his hands and headed for the door. "I'm leaving. Like I said, I have a flight to catch with Junie and my beautiful girlfriend. I've said what I had to say."

Briana broke down in tears, burying her face in her hands pitifully, as Bryson pushed past Ashton's much thinner frame. When he got to the door, he looked back and scowled, "And let this be your first and final warning. If Junie ever tells me you've put your hands on her, or if I even think you've looked at her the wrong way, I'll be all over you like flies on barbeque. Do I make myself clear? Stay away from her, and keep your hands off of Briana. I expect to never see you again, if you know what's good for you."

Bryson slammed the door, and fished around in his pocket for a pair of sunglasses. It was a record high for December with temperatures nearing the 60s and the sun beaming brightly, melting any little bit of snow that the Midwest had conjured up. He breathed in the fresh air, allowing his lungs to gather in as much as it could, before shuffling down the steps.

He went to his car, climbed inside, and took off towards his apartment. Now that that was taken care of and his mind was clear, he could focus on relaxation and making two of his favorite people happy.

Orlando was as beautiful as they expected it to be. Its palm trees were full and inviting, the weather was warm and sticky, and every tourist milling about was excited with impending Christmas cheer. Extravagant decorations, rotund Christmas trees, and bright lights seemed to fill every restaurant, store, and home that their rental truck passed as they headed out for a late dinner.

Jet lagged but still ecstatic to be in "Mickey's town," Junie talked nonstop as she pointed out different landmarks, billboards, and cool city treasures. She couldn't wait to visit all of the different amusement parks and famous studios, and see her favorite Disney characters. She especially kept her eye out for Princess Tiana, Moana, and Tinkerbell.

They settled at an Italian restaurant that

served delicious food and was one of the many spots that Bryson frequented whenever his family travelled to Orlando. Junie and Bryson ordered a 14-inch specialty pizza with pepperoni, black olives, mushrooms, and onions, and a mozzarella-filled crust. Camryn chose a pasta dish with blackened chicken and two garlic sticks. Bryson reached over and helped himself to one of them before she could fully spread her napkin on her lap and dig in.

"Sure, help yourself to more carbs," she teased.

"Hey, we're on vacation. There are no diets, no weight watching, and no calorie counting. Let me enjoy myself, woman." He winked, taking a big bite out of the garlicky goodness. Junie giggled.

They ate in silence for a few moments, other than the sounds of surrounding chatter, light music, and the bustle of the semi-busy restaurant. Junie devoured three slices before begging to go off and dance by the live band with the other children, leaving Camryn and Bryson alone. He stared at her.

She wiped her mouth free of tomato sauce and eyed him skeptically. "What's wrong? Do I have food in my teeth?"

"No, not at all. You look fine. You *are* fine," he reiterated. "So fine I wanna make ya mine," he rhymed.

"You're as cheesy as this Parmesan." She motioned to the glass container of cheese.

"Oh yeah? Well, you won't find the gift I got you cheesy."

"Wait, you got me a gift?" Camryn's voice raised a little and then she sighed, "Bryson, I told you no gifts. The plane ticket and invite to Orlando was more than enough."

He shrugged and gave her a bored look. "When have I ever listened in life?"

She lightly kicked him under the table. "You listen to me, I hope."

"Eh, when you're kissing me, yes. But other than that, it goes in one ear and out the other," he joked, immediately bracing himself for what was to come.

She didn't disappoint and reached over to swat his shoulder.

"I'm kidding, I'm kidding," he rushed to say. "But seriously, I know that you said no gifts, but I couldn't help it when I thought about this particular gift. I had to give it to you, and you *will* receive it…tomorrow morning."

Camryn pressed her lips together and studied him. He wasn't backing down, and only threw back a cute little grin that she found irresistible. Reluctantly, she exhaled again and smiled. "Alright, Bryson. I will accept your gift and be grateful while doing so, but know that I didn't bring anything other than myself."

"Hey." He placed his hands over his heart. "That's the only gift I need, baby. That's the *only* gift I really want."

"Oh, yeah?" She smiled warmly, angling her head to eye him sweetly, and batted her eyelashes. She leaned in a bit, lowering her voice so that it was sultry. "You know the ONLY gift I want and need?"

He leaned closer, grabbing her hands in his. "What's that, beautiful?"

She leaned the remainder of the way, lifting up with her weight on her arms, until their lips were nearly pressed together. She licked her lips and the motion caused his mouth to twitch slightly. He blinked, she blinked, and then finally, she whispered, "Mmm. The only gift I'd like TONIGHT is some yummy…"

He leaned in closer.

"*Hot…*"

His mouth hung open.

"Rich, sweet, and tasty…"

Bryson's eyebrows shot up.

"…butter pecan ice cream with fudge and a cherry on top. Oooh, Bry-baby, that would set my Christmas off just right!"

His jaw went slack and he began to choke. She couldn't keep her face straight and burst into a fight of giggles as she sat back down and threw her head back against the leather booth. He watched her chuckle and it was obvious how hard he was trying not to join in or at least crack a smile.

"Oh. That's cold," Bryson murmured, pretending to be agitated. "That's just wrong."

"I'm kidding! Well, no, I *do* want butter pecan ice cream with fudge and cherries," she winked, still laughing, "but I couldn't resist. You looked so cute while you were trying to figure out what I wanted."

Bryson pretended to be hurt for a few more minutes before pulling out his wallet and calling for Junie. He flagged down the waitress, paid off the bill and then tipped the young lady generously.

"Ready?" He looked from Junie to Camryn and back again.

They both nodded.

"Let's roll, ladies." He smiled and headed to an ice cream parlor further down the street, honoring Camryn's request with her butter pecan ice cream, fudge, and cherries, and sharing a banana split with Junie.

"So where to next?" Junie asked, licking her mouth and chin free of sprinkles and custard.

Bryson grabbed her hand and squeezed it as they headed out to the truck. "Next...we're going to go back to the resort and get some rest."

Junie pouted, looking around at the other children and their families. "*Bed?* Already? I thought we were on vacation," she whined. "Why can't I stay up and walk around like the rest of the little kids?"

Camryn giggled as Bryson found the right words to say. "Stop frowning, baby girl. We have a big day tomorrow, remember? It's Christmas. We're going to get up really early and have breakfast with Mickey and the gang, and then you can open your gifts. The quicker you go to bed, the sooner Santa will come and deliver your presents."

"Oh, yeah! I keep forgetting Santa's coming!" Her mood seemed to do a complete 180-degree turn as she jumped up and down in place. "Can we see him riding on his sleigh? How will he know which way to go since we're not at home? What if he forgets what I asked for?"

Bryson's smile slipped a little at the frantic questions, as Camryn continued to giggle behind a hand. He looked over at her for help, but she closed her eyes and turned away, laughing even harder.

"Thanks a lot," he mumbled, and then leaned down to Junie's eye level.

By now, the little girl's chin was quivering.

"Baby girl, calm down. Listen to me and look at me. Santa knows *everything*. He knows where every little girl or boy lives and keeps track of them. Trust me, you have been nice all year, so he knows exactly where to find you and where to drop off your gifts. That's why we have to get to bed. So he can have enough time to get to everyone on time."

"Before Rudolph and the other reindeer go to bed?" she asked. "He won't come unless we go to sleep, huh, Uncle B?"

"Exactly. That's exactly right." He gave her a high-five, and then stood up to his full height, brushing his fingertips across her soft hair. They closed in on the truck and climbed in. When everyone was buckled in, Bryson pulled off and looked at Junie in the rearview. "So once we go back to the hotel, you and Camryn can run a bath, and you can get washed up and go to sleep. I'll let you buy a movie on the TV and you can even drink a cup of hot chocolate, but you have to promise me you'll try to go to sleep after that."

"I promise," she vowed, as a yawn worked itself from her mouth.

Bryson looked over at Camryn knowingly. They were barely slipping the room key in the door and getting situated, when Junie settled in her bedroom and fell asleep almost instantly. Camryn slipped inside of the room and helped her out of her clothes and into a nightshirt.

Bryson took a quick shower and then made his way back outside into the warm night, a fresh rain on the horizon, and the beautiful sunset becoming more and more pronounced. He looked out into the distance, the beautiful city and streetlights flickering, the oversized palm tree leaves blowing, and flashes of red and white from cars occasionally grabbing his attention. He breathed in the scent of the atmosphere, thanking God for seeing another Christmas, being able to share the holiday with his niece, and now a woman who he cared for deeply. Things moved quickly, namely his feelings and their relationship, but he was never more excited or sure about someone.

Camryn was the picture of perfection, and though he realized *no one* was without flaw, she was pretty close to it. He couldn't get enough of her, and didn't want to. He was so wrapped up in his thoughts and the beauty of the night that he didn't hear Camryn approach him from behind until she cleared her throat softly.

He whipped around and took her in, his breath catching. She had been wearing a dressier outfit for dinner, but was now comfortable in a robe with a visible camisole and silky shorts underneath. On her feet were fuzzy slippers, and her hair had been pinned up to display her collarbone and delicate neck. She leaned casually into the doorframe, one foot out on the balcony, the other propped back in the room, and in her hand was the chilled bottle of sparkling apple cider they requested during check-in. In her other hand were two glass flutes.

"Hey," he greeted, his eyes skimming over her. He leaned with his lower back pressed into the railing, keeping his feet apart for leverage, and then resting his elbows back onto the railing.

"Hey." She grinned and stepped fully out onto the balcony, careful to untangle her body from the curtains before she slid the thick glass door closed. "I know you wanted to drink this on the actual holiday with Junie, but I figured we could get a head start since it's almost midnight. We can sip a little and toast to our first Christmas together."

A tender smile tugged at his lips. "Hopefully it won't be our last."

"It won't be," she countered, biting her bottom lip shyly. "Because no matter what happens, I want us to always stay in touch and be honest with each other. I want to always be your friend."

"Can I be honest with you?" He accepted the glass and the bottle of tasty, nonalcoholic drink. "I can't promise you that, baby. I can't promise to always be your friend."

"Oh?"

Bryson shook his head slowly back and forth, pouring them each a generous amount and then setting the bottle down on the small table wedged between the patio furniture. "No, I can't."

"Why's that?"

"It won't work," he said simply.

She genuinely looked troubled, searching his eyes. "Why not? Why can't it work?"

He pulled her with his available hand to stand directly in front of him, wrapping his arm around her waist protectively, and then swaying their bodies left and right. They sipped silently after clinking their glasses once, their minds going in opposite directions. She seemed to still be looking for an answer, and he was searching for the right words to say.

Finally, after draining the last of his beverage, he deposited their empty glasses on the table, and then reclaimed her body in his arms. Humming absently, he nestled his face in the crook of her neck. She sighed as he made a meal out of her skin—nipping here, kissing there.

"It won't work, Camryn Young, because friends can't be attracted and infatuated with one another. It won't work for a number of reasons, really," he explained and rubbed his nose against the side of her neck. "'Cause of things like this." He brushed his lips against the sensitive skin below her ear, and smiled at the way she shuddered. "'Cause I love kissing you. 'Cause I can't get enough of you. 'Cause I never want to let you go, and let some other unworthy man have you."

Camryn turned in his arms, hearing the sincerity and seriousness in his voice. She slid her hands up his body, resting them at his shoulders for a moment, and then moving them up to the back of his head where she cradled his face lovingly.

Bryson kept his eyes on her but turned his head to kiss the insides of her wrists. "That's not going to work for me. I don't know about you, but I can't let the woman I love be *just* a friend. You're too special, too sweet, and too beautiful. I wouldn't last a day with that title."

Camryn's eyes widened; her breaths deepened, and the grip on his head grew stronger and snugger. He watched her eyelashes flutter, touching the tops of her cheeks, before a single tear slid from her eye.

"You—you *love* me?"

He brushed a few stray hairs away from her forehead. "I love you, Camryn. I love everything about you, but mostly, I love your heart. I love the way you can be yourself with me, and I can be myself with you. I love the way you think; I love your passions, and what makes you happy. I love the way you are such a positive example to Junie, and I love—YOU—the woman. You're beautiful; you've managed to work your way into my heart at a time that I didn't think possible. Whether you feel as strongly as I do or not, I couldn't let another day pass without telling you."

Camryn dropped her head, misty-eyed and overwhelmed.

He lifted her head back up. "So consider this the Christmas gift I couldn't wait to give you. It's *the only gift* I could think of that you deserved more than anything else in this world. Unconditional love."

"Bryson."

"Whether you feel the same way or not, I also want you to know…"

"Bryson…"

"…I vow to make you a happy woman, if you think we have a chance. I want you to continue to trust me and…"

She laughed and cut him off, "I love you too, baby! I love *you*. Now, shut up and kiss me," she growled.

Bryson chuckled, licking his lips, and dipping his head. "Yes…ma'am!"

As they continued to kiss and seal their professed love for one another, the sliding door opened behind them.

Junie appeared, rubbing her eyes, and looking sluggish but hopeful.

"Did Santa come yet?"

Camryn smiled and stepped to the side, while Bryson pulled his niece into his arms. He knelt down. "Yes, baby girl, and since it *is* almost Christmas, I'll let you open up one gift, okay?"

Sleepiness was no longer an option as she jumped up and down in place and then looked at the adults in excitement.

"Oooh, thank you! Thank you!"

Bryson headed inside to grab one of the smaller, hidden gifts from his bag, and Junie leaned on the railing next to Camryn. "Will you open up a gift too, Miss Foster?"

Camryn's wide smile faded into a softer one. She watched Bryson through the glass door and shook her head. Then she looked down at the inquisitive young girl beside her, who, right along with her uncle, had also stolen her heart.

"No, honey. I've already unwrapped my present, and it was everything I could have ever prayed for."

THE END

Thank you for reading! **Please consider leaving a review on Amazon/Goodreads, and/or write to the author herself at** *info@osrbooks.com.* Reviews and word-of-mouth recommendations mean EVERYTHING to the author.

If you are discussing this short story as a book club, please refer to the below questions.

1. If you were in Camryn's shoes, would you have revealed your identity and secrets, despite knowing Bryson previously?

2. Was Camryn wrong for suggesting that Junie could possibly be involved in domestic abuse? Did she overstep her boundaries?

3. Could/would you have uprooted and started over like Camryn?

ABOUT THE AUTHOR

Olivia Shaw-Reel has written nearly 30 books before her 30th birthday. Her award-winning novels, *Soul Cry, What God Has Joined Together, and Matters of the Hart: A Tale of the Dysfunctional Hart Sisters*, have become her biggest-selling books to date.

She also hosts *The Reel Love Podcast* with her husband, Paris. Olivia lives in Milwaukee, WI.

Visit the official storefront for updates and to purchase autographed paperbacks at *osrbooks.com.*

Follow her on Instagram and Facebook at *@oliviashawreel.*

OTHER TITLES FROM THE AUTHOR

Soul Cry, Vol. 3

What God Has Joined Together, *2-Book Series*

Baptized in Her Seduction: A Church Love Affair, *2-Book Series*

Lord, Save Me From Myself, *2-Book Series*

Meet Me at the Altar

Full Court Mess

Andrue & Sy'mone: An Urban Love Affair, *3-Book Series*

Can't Leave Him Alone After the Love We Made, *Book 1*

Sins of a Mafia Princess

Matters of the Hart: A Tale of the Dysfunctional Hart Sisters, *3-Book Series*

Stuck Wit'chu

In Love With Everything You Could Be

Stalked by My Pastor, *Book 1*

A Christmas Miracle

Who's Loving You This Christmas?

Saved, Sanctified, & Filled With Anxiety Compilation

Olivia Shaw-Reel

www.ingramcontent.com/pod-product-compliance
Lightning Source LLC
Chambersburg PA
CBHW050358030726
47503CB00006B/1916